THE

PLAYLIST

A Novel by

E. Nigma

To submit a manuscript for our review,

email us at

submissions@majorkeypublishing.com

Change can be a scary thing. Sometimes you may feel that nobody in the world understands what you're going through or that you're alone with it all. Change is difficult, but sometimes change comes with a purpose. Sometimes, we're forced into change for personal growth. Sometimes, change is for the better.

This is dedicated to those out there who were forced into difficult situations, but overcame their fears and made the best out of it anyway. This also dedicated to growing up and finding love. Sometimes it's not who you think it is.

Chapter 1

The Love I Never Had (NKOTB - Please Don't Go Girl) - 1990

The clock has just struck noon in Fort Riley Middle School, setting off the bell for lunch. The puberty-filled adolescents quickly fill the school hallway heading in various directions, laughing and joking with their peers. The school itself is typical in the early 90s, just a little cleaner being that's it's located on an army base.

Walking down the hallway with a couple of friends throughout the crowd is Ken, who is holding a couple of books joking with two of his friends. One of the friends split from Ken and his best friend, Gilbert, as they both make it to Ken's locker.

"So, how you think you did on Mr. Haynes's test?" The pudgy Gilbert asks his friend while running his hand through his jet-black hair.

Ken opens his locker as he shakes his head.

"Probably failed," Ken admits. "I don't think we even went over all that stuff on that test."

"Well, I didn't have to worry about it. I copied off Jessica's paper. She normally aces these things," Gilbert admits with a slick grin.

Ken scratches his high-top fade before placing his books in his locker.

"Are you going to eat today?" Gilbert asks.

"I don't know. I'm not really that hungry, to be honest," Ken answers as he takes a look at several of the passing females in his grade with a smirk.

Both he and Gilbert are in the seventh grade, which meant that their hormones were running wild. Girls started to stand out more and more as the year progressed. While Gilbert adjusted well during this puberty transition, Ken is still struggling to adjust to his newfound attraction to the opposite sex.

Gilbert notices his lanky friend's wandering eyes and shakes his hand.

"Why don't you just go talk to one of them?" he says, snapping Ken out of his gaze.

"What are you talking about?" Ken questions.

"Come on! All you do is sit there and look at girls. It's

probably why you failed that test," Gilbert points out. "Why you act so scared all the time? Girls aren't gonna bite you, you know."

Ken shakes his head when he suddenly notices a couple of the school bullies walking through the hallway towards them. He quickly covers his crotch as Gilbert continues to ridicule him.

"How are you ever gonna get a girlfriend if you're scared to talk to girls?" Gilbert continues.

"Gil, you better-"

"No, don't try and change the subject," Gilbert interrupts. "I'm gonna start thinking you like the guys more than the ladies if you keep this up."

"Dude, I'm just trying to-"

"That's why you let Jody get away from you at the dance," Gilbert states, hitting a nerve with Ken.

Jody was the one girl Ken was close to getting the courage to ask to dance with him during the winter dance several weeks ago. Just as he was about to ask her, another one of his classmates asked her to dance. Now because of that, the two are now a couple, which frustrated Ken. He didn't sleep for days knowing he missed his shot to have his first official girlfriend. It is especially hard for Ken because he was black in a predominantly white school. The few black females that attended the school normally find themselves with the school athletes, not an unpopular quiet teen like himself.

Still, that Jody comment irritates Ken, and he remains silent while Gilbert laughs at him.

"I mean, you know Jody and Kevin are going together, right?" Gilbert continues while laughing. "It could have been you. All you had to do is-"

Gilbert is silenced as one of the bullies quickly moves in and punches him in the crotch, sending him falling to the ground grimacing in pain. The bully looks at Ken, and notices he's guarded before laughing and running off. Gilbert looks up and notices Ken is guarded as well with a smirk on his face.

"I tried to tell you," Ken says with a grin.

"Okay, okay. I… I deserved that," Gilbert says while gritting his teeth.

Ken looks around for several moments before letting

his guard down and helping his friend up.

Gilbert bends over, trying to catch his breath, as Ken watches the bullies from a distance punch several other students in their crotch.

"I told you that you have to be careful during lunchtime," Ken says. "Ball tag isn't a game you take lightly. You could get some serious damage."

"This has been going on for months!" Gilbert exclaims as he stands straight, still in pain. "When does it end?"

"Well, my guess is since those are eight graders, the game will end at the end of this year," Ken answers. "Until then, my friend, hands on your balls at all times, or maybe ask your parents to buy you a cup."

Gilbert straightens up once more, and he and Ken make their way down the hall. Gilbert walks with a noticeable limp as Ken chuckles to himself.

In the lunchroom, Gilbert and Ken take a seat at an unoccupied table after getting their food from the lunch line. Gilbert takes his milk carton and places it on his crotch causing Ken to burst into laughter.

"I was wondering why you didn't get a Hi-C today," Ken says with a chuckle.

"All the good flavors were gone anyway," Gilbert replies as he begins eating his food. "I mean,

if you know everyone likes the orange, why don't you make more of the orange? Just doesn't make sense to me."

"Stop complaining. I used to go to a school where that milk you have on your balls was the only option you had to drink," Ken points out. "And we also didn't have the option for Pizza Hut pizza, just a cardboard square pizza."

"You're lying," Gilbert says with a smirk. "What school you ever went to like that? Compton?"

"Nope. New Orleans," Ken responds before taking a sip of his drink.

He spent his fourth-grade year at a public school in New Orleans. It wasn't as clean or privileged as the schools on the military bases. To him, it was the single worst year of his life and still gave him nightmares.

"Yeah right," Gilbert says before taking a bite of his pizza. "You never lived in any place like that. Everyone knows that Compton is the worse place in the world, and you have never lived in Compton."

Ken shakes his head as he starts looking around the cafeteria. Ever since 'Boyz in the Hood' came out in the theaters, kids in his school thought that Compton was the worst place in the world to live. It didn't help when two brothers from Compton joined their school a couple of months ago. Everyone is scared of them, but Ken knew that there were a lot of other places like that scattered throughout the states.

Gilbert notices his friend looking around the cafeteria and smiles.

"Looking for your made-up girlfriend, aren't you?" He says.

"What?"

"I know you're looking for Sharon," Gilbert responds. "What you gonna do when you find her? Just look at her, just like every other day."

"Shut up," an irritated Ken responds as he begins eating his pizza.

"I mean, that's all you do. Tell me I'm wrong," Gilbert responds with a mouth full of pizza.

"Why are we always talking about me?" Ken questions. "What about you? Who is your girlfriend?"

"I told you she doesn't go to this school," Gilbert responds, causing Ken to smirk.

A girlfriend who doesn't go to the same school as him was a convenient lie in Ken's mind. Typical middle school chatter to make someone feel they're more of an adult than others around them.

Ken shakes his head when he notices Sharon walking into the cafeteria with her friends. He is mesmerized as he watches her get into the lunch line gossiping with her classmates. *Sharon's smile could light up anyone's day,*

Ken thinks to himself as he admires her from afar. Her blonde shoulder-length hair sways with her every movement as the lip-gloss she was wearing was almost perfect. She is the type of girl that puts her makeup on after her parents drop her off to avoid them knowing of her sinister deed. It made her feel grown, and it attracted many guys, including Ken.

Gilbert looks up from his meal, notices Ken gazing at Sharon, and shakes his head with disappointment.

"Dude, this is getting old," he says while finishing his meal. "I mean, we talked about seventh grade being our year last summer, remember? You said this would be the year you would have a girlfriend. What happened?"

Ken sighs as he takes a sip of his drink, trying to figure that out himself.

"I don't know," he answers. "I guess, maybe... I don't know."

Ken looks over towards Sharon once more as the two share a look with each other. Both were interested in each other, but neither knew how to communicate it. They kept eye contact with each other until Sharon reached the front of the line and grabbed her tray. It was the highlight of Ken's day to have those eye contact connections with his crush.

Gilbert, on the other hand, is embarrassed for his friend and shakes his head, mocking Ken's infatuation.

"Sad, just sad," he says. "You know I can talk to Brianna and see if she can set you up with her."

"Absolutely not," Ken snaps back.

"Why not?"

"Because I don't want to, okay," Ken replies.

Before Gilbert can respond, he notices Brianna, who is standing in front of Sharon in the lunch line paying for her food. He admires the flowing brunette hair down her back, and even though she had a mouth full of braces, her dimples when she smiled was alluring to him. He also likes her freckles, which he always envisions himself playing connect the dots on her face. Before she's able to walk off, Gilbert jumps up with a flirtatious smile on his face, blocking her path.

"Bri, what's up?" he says to an unbothered Brianna.

"Gilbert," she softly replies.

"Hey, I was just seeing how you were doing?" Gilbert continues with a smirk.

Brianna frowns, waiting for him to get to the point. While Gilbert thought she was cute, she had nothing but hatred towards him. Brianna was Gilbert's first official girlfriend at the beginning of the school year. They were together for about a month, which in middle school is the equivalent of several years. The two had an awful break up at the Back to School dance when Gilbert was caught dancing with another female. It wasn't intentional as he didn't think Brianna was coming to the dance, but he was quickly surprised by her presence. Since then, Gilbert has only been with his alleged girlfriend from another school.

Before the two could continue, Sharon walks over and taps Brianna on the shoulder.

"Hey, I'm going to go get us a seat," she says before looking at Gilbert. "Hey, Gilbert."

"Hey, Sharon. I was just talking about you," he responds with a smile.

"Oh really? About?"

Gilbert notices Ken out of the corner of his eyes, shaking his head and decides to keep their conversation a secret for the moment.

"Nothing important. Just that you're the only person I know with blue eyes," he says, chuckling.

Sharon rolls her eyes before looking towards Ken.

"Hey," she softly spoke.

Ken opens his mouth to respond, but nothing comes out. He instead nods his head, much to his embarrassment. Sharon smiles at him before making her way off to the other side of the cafeteria.

Gilbert turns his attention back towards Brianna, who is still frowning at him.

"What do you want, Gilbert?" she asks. "My food is getting cold."

"That it is. Hey, listen, my homebody Ken here likes your girl Sharon. Anything you can do to set them up?" Gilbert responds, stunning Ken.

Brianna looks at Ken with a smile on her face.

"He does? Oh my god, that is so cute," she says, as Ken nervously looks on, still stunned by Gilbert's words.

"I know, it really is," Gilbert replies with a big smile on his face. "So, what can you do to help him out? Does she like him too?"

Ken is quiet as every last bit of his existence hinges on her response to that question.

"I don't know. She mentioned once that he's cute, but I don't know if she likes him as a boyfriend or not," Brianna answers.

Ken's heart almost explodes in happiness, hearing that, not only did Sharon talk about him, but mentioned the fact that he's cute. That was more than enough praise from her as far as he was concerned.

"Cool, so back to my first question. Can you set him up?" Gilbert repeats.

Brianna thinks for a few moments before nodding her head with approval.

"Hey, this is gonna sound crazy, but why don't you two come to our friendship bracelet class after school?" Brianna suggests. "Me and her are both in it. I can set them up there."

Gilbert cringes, hearing that plan.

"Friendship bracelet class?" He replies. "Isn't that just for girls?"

"No jerk," Brianna snaps back. "Tim is in there, and Maurice comes in every now and then. Look, if you want me to set you up, be in Ms. Hardy's room after school."

Gilbert nods his head with agreement while Ken is filled with nervousness.

"We'll be there," Gilbert responds. "Now, let's talk about us, and where we went wrong?"

The smile on Brianna's face quickly fades as she

frowns at her ex once more.

"In your dreams. Besides, you have your made-up girlfriend from another school you're going with now," Brianna responds before walking off.

"She's not made up! She's real!" Gilbert exclaims to Brianna before taking a seat across from his friend. "Don't know why everyone keeps saying that!"

He glances over towards Ken and notices the rage in his friend's eyes.

"You seem like something's bothering you," Gilbert nonchalantly says as Ken can no longer hold it in.

"Are you out of your mind?!" He exclaims. "I just told you I didn't want you to ask Brianna to set me up! It wasn't even a full two minutes before you did the very thing I asked you not to do!"

"I did it for your own good," Gilbert fires back. "Besides, if it wasn't for me, you wouldn't know that Sharon thought you were cute."

Ken backs down a bit knowing his friend was right. He still is fearful of talking to Sharon about his feelings. Gilbert notices his friend is tense and tries to calm him down.

"Relax. The hard part is over," Gilbert says. "You see, I know girls, and the thing about them is that they are easy to control. I just planted the seed about you liking Sharon. You think Brianna is gonna keep that to herself? She ran right over there and told Sharon what we just were talking about. I promise you. When we get to the class, it'll be a piece of cake."

Ken looks at his friend strangely.

"You know girls? Weren't you the one being chased by Brianna at the Back to School dance? The same girl you claim to know?" Ken points out.

"Never said I never made a mistake or two," Gilbert retorts. "Besides, that wasn't my fault."

"Whatever you say. All I know is I never saw a fat kid run that fast in my life," Ken responds with a chuckle. "She almost caught you."

"Yeah, yeah, whatever," Gilbert says as the two continued to go back and forth with each other.

Just before class dismissal later that day, Ken is a

nervous wreck sitting in the back of his English class, looking at the clock over the chalkboard. His stomach is bubbling, and he's almost hyperventilating watching the clock about to strike three, knowing what he needed to do after school. He can feel his heart racing, and it increases once he hears the dismissal bell.

The classroom quickly clears out as Ken remains in his seat, shaking from the nervousness overtaking his senses. His teacher, Ms. Kurth, notices he's still in the class and can tell something's not right.

"Ken, are you okay?" she asks.

"Huh? Oh yeah. I'm fine, Ms. Kurth," Ken says, snapping out of his thoughts. "Just a little under the weather, that's all."

"Do you need to go to the nurse's office?"

"Oh, no, it's nothing like that. I'll be fine," Ken says as he nervously begins to pack his things.

Ms. Kurth looks on with concern and is about to approach her student when a smiling Gilbert pokes his head in the class.

"Hello, Ms. Kurth," he says cheerfully.

"Hello, Gilbert," she responds. "Did you need something?"

"No, I'm just fine," he answers, walking into the class. "I'm just here picking up my friend Ken."

Gilbert walks over to Ken's desk, ready to lead him to victory. He thought Ken might try to sneak out and head home. He was determined to make sure his friend made it to the after school class to get with the girl of his dreams.

"You ready to go?" he asks.

Ken sighs before grabbing his backpack from the ground. Ms. Kurth is still concerned as she approaches Ken.

"Ken, are you sure you're okay?" she asks.

"Yes, Ms. Kurth. I'm fine," he answers before he and Gilbert make their way out of the room.

Once they're in the hallway, an excited Gilbert pats his friend on the back, trying to hype him up.

"This is gonna be the defining moment of your life," he says. "By the end of the day, you're going to be going with Sharon Miller. Do you realize what this means for you?"

Ken doesn't hear Gilbert's words. He's completely zoned out as fear overwhelms him.

Twenty minutes later, Ken, Gilbert, Sharon, Brianna, and several other students, including the handsome looking Tim, are all lying on several beanbags in the middle of the class working on their friendship bracelets. Ken and Gilbert are sharing one beanbag, and Brianna and Sharon are sharing one just across from them. The tops of the bracelets are safety-pinned to their jeans as they weave their bracelets. Gilbert is frustrated as he struggles to put his together, much to Brianna's delight.

"You're doing it wrong, stupid," she says, bringing the group's attention to his struggles. "You have to loop it like a four."

"Well, I'm sorry if I'm not the bracelet guru that you are," Gilbert grumbles as he starts his thread over.

After a few moments of silence, Gilbert nods to Brianna, who smiles as she turns to Sharon.

"So, Sharon, what's up with you?" she asks her friend, who is stealing glimpses of Ken when she can.

"Nothing," Sharon responds. "Why?"

"I don't know. You just seem a little quiet, that's all."

"I'm just sitting here getting my bracelets done, that's-
"

"Oh my God, I can't take this anymore," an impatient Gilbert responds, cutting Sharon off. "Look, let's be honest here. I've seen how you and my homeboy Ken here look at each other all day every day. I mean, you two look at each other during lunch, assemblies, and even at Ken's sister's cheerleader practices. You two might as well be boyfriend and girlfriend, don't you agree?"

Ken is stunned as he looks at his friend with his eyes wide open. Sharon turns red with embarrassment as Brianna scowls at her former boyfriend.

"Are you crazy?" Brianna replies. "This is you letting me set them up?"

"You were taking too long," Gilbert responds, turning his attention back to Sharon. "So how 'bout it? You two are going to go together or what?"

The group is quiet as Sharon slowly nods her head.

"Sure, I can do that," she says, giving Ken the answer

he's been waiting a lifetime for.

Gilbert smiles as he turns his attention towards his friend.

"You see! I told you!" he replies, congratulating his friend. "I mean, who else was there? Unless you wanted to go with Tim over there."

Sharon thinks for a few moments before nodding her head.

"I could go with Tim," she replies, stunning Ken and confusing Tim, who is leaning on a nearby beanbag next to the crew.

"Um… Okay, I guess," Tim answers solidifying their new relationship.

Ken is devastated as he struggles to hold himself together. Brianna and Gilbert are stunned as another student close by chimes in on the situation laughing at Ken.

"Damn, dude. She broke up with you real quick," he says.

"What are you talking about? We weren't going together," Ken fires back.

"If you say so," the student replies before going back

to his bracelet.

Sharon walks over and joins Tim on his beanbag as the two starts talking with each other. A heartbroken Ken continues to work on his bracelet in silence while Gilbert and Brianna are still trying to figure out what just happened.

Twenty minutes later, Ken is rushing outside the school when Gilbert rushes to catch up with him.

"Ken, I'm sorry. I didn't know this would happen," he pleads with his friend. "I thought this was a sure thing."

"Don't worry about it," Ken says, walking down the street. "It's not your fault."

"Ken, please. I feel bad, man. I don't know what else to say."

Ken stops and turns to his friend, trying to keep from crying as best he can.

"Sometimes things just don't work out," he says. "It wasn't your fault. It wasn't my fault. It wasn't Tim's fault. Things just happen, and you can't control them. Look, I gotta go. I'll see you tomorrow."

Ken quickly turns off and starts walking down the street once more. Tears slowly make their way down his face as the rejection is too much for him to handle. All he's ever wanted is a girlfriend to call his own, and for a brief moment, he had exactly what he wanted before it was cruelly snatched from him.

A couple of weeks later, at the DYA, which is middle school local hangout, the school is having a dance for their students. The gym area has been converted over to a dance floor. The DJ is at the far end of the gym area playing music. While the concession stand and the lounging portion of the DYA remain largely the same with added dance streamer decorations for the event.

Leaning on the wall just outside of the dance floor is Ken, who seems disinterested in what's going on around him. He observes several couples laughing and joking with each other and shakes his head in disgust, sick of seeing others happy in their relationships. He also watches a couple of the younger sixth-graders playing tag and running around the gym. He rolls his eyes as he felt that was beneath him as a seventh-grader.

Gilbert has arrived at the dance and quickly makes his way over to him as Ken chuckles at his outfit.

"What in the world are you dressed in?" Ken says with a chuckle. "You look like you're on an episode of Miami Vice!"

Ken is referring to Gilbert's Don Johnson like appearance complete with a white blazer, t-shirt, and matching white pants. His hair is also slicked back, finishing the look. Gilbert dismisses his friend's critique of him.

"Dude, whatever," he responds. "This outfit is cool. Much cooler than the simple school day outfit you're wearing."

Ken shakes his head as he turns his attention back towards the dancefloor. Gilbert leans back on the wall as well while checking out the atmosphere.

"Why you over here by yourself anyway?" Gilbert asks.

"I'm just hangin', I guess," Ken answers.

"You're supposed to be having a good time." Gilbert

checks out a few of the girls walking by. "I mean, look at all these girls! How can you not enjoy yourself with all this?"

"I see them," Ken replies. "Lots of couples here too."

"Couples? Like who?" Gilbert asks before Ken points out Tim and Sharon arriving through the main exit.

"Well, them for starters," he says, watching them greet a few people on their way in.

"Oh, damn. I didn't see them," Gilbert responds, still feeling a little responsible for the fiasco that happened weeks ago between Ken and Sharon. "Hey, look, I know you said we're cool and all, but I still feel like crap with all that-"

"Dude, it's alright," Ken responds, cutting him off. "Trust me, I'm over it. I'm no drag."

Gilbert nods his head when he notices Shannon, a classmate of theirs, making her way into the building. His eyes light up as a smile grows on his face.

"My girl Shannon is in the building," an excited Gilbert says, confusing Ken.

"Your girl?" he quips. "Your girl since when? I thought

she was with Ben."

"Broke up last week, my good friend," Gilbert responds. "You need to keep up with your hallway gossip. Anyway, their split up was my gain."

Ken nods his head, impressed with his friend.

"Well, congratulations," he responds. "Now, you can stop going around talking about your fake girlfriend that goes to another school."

Gilbert chuckles while shaking his head.

"Dude, whatever. One day you're gonna meet Carissa for real. Then how dumb are you gonna feel," Gilbert fires back.

"I thought her name was Sonja?" Ken points out.

"It doesn't matter," Gilbert quickly responds as he straightens out his blazer. "How do I look?"

"Like a fool," Ken jokes as Gilbert shakes his head.

"Says the guy holding up the wall," Gilbert fires back.

"True. So true," Ken replies with a smirk. "Good luck."

Gilbert gives his friend thumbs up before rushing off to meet with Shannon. The two share a brief hug before making their way towards the lounging area.

Ken sighs as he quietly watches Tim and Sharon laugh and joke with a few friends on the dance floor. Sharon catches a glimpse of Ken from a distance making eye contact with him. Ken nods his head to her acknowledging that he sees her. A small smile enters her face as she nods back at him before going back to her conversation with her friends.

A few moments later, the gym fills with music from New Kids on the Block. Please Don't Go, Girl has the couples in the gym heading to the middle of the dancefloor. Ken watches Gilbert and Shannon dancing and chuckles to himself when Gilbert makes eye contact with him and gives him a thumbs up. Watching Sharon and Tim dancing, however, wasn't as pleasurable. Tim holding and dancing with his girl because of his lack of confidence, irks him. He was dancing with his girl, and as the song continues, Ken realizes he's not over it as much as he thought he was.

Sharon catches a glimpse of him once more and notices his reaction to her and Tim. After a few moments, Ken walks off towards the lounging area. His heart is still broken, and he couldn't torment himself any longer with it. He's about to take a seat at an unoccupied area when one of the six graders who was running around playing tag, taps him on his arm.

"You're it!" the sixth-grader yells before running off.

Ken frowns at the immaturity of the sixth-grader. Still, after a few moments, a sinister smile enters his face as he runs off chasing the sixth-grader and others who are in the game. He was able to let go of his pain for a while longer while just being a kid again.

A couple of weeks later, at the end of a grueling school day, Ken is walking to his locker with his books when he notices several of his classmates, including Brianna, gathered around Sharon's locker looking at her with sadness in their eyes. Ken drops his books in his locker as he tries to figure out what's going on. Brianna starts to walk off when Ken notices she has tears in her eyes.

"Brianna, what's going on?" Ken asks as he walks up to her.

"You didn't hear?" Brianna responds with tears still streaming down her face. "Sharon's moving. Her dad was stationed in Colorado. This is her last day."

Ken is caught off guard with the news as he looks in Sharon's direction.

"Wow, no... I... I didn't know," he says.

"I can't believe it," Brianna says before rushing off, still upset with the news.

A saddened Ken shakes his head when he notices the group around Sharon walk off, leaving her alone. He takes a deep breath as he makes his way over to her locker as she collects her things.

"Hey," he says, startling her slightly.

"Hey."

"I just heard. Colorado. Wow," Ken says, trying to overcome his fears of speaking with girls.

"I know. I'm gonna miss everybody," Sharon says. "In a whole new city by myself without any friends. I don't know what I'm gonna do with myself."

"You'll make friends, what are you talking about?" Ken responds. "I mean, you're like one of the most popular girls in seventh grade. I'm sure you'll be on the top of the Colorado popular list in no time."

Sharon smiles as Ken's words mean a lot to her. In the couple years that they've known each other, this was the most they had ever spoken. She closes her locker for one last time as the two share an awkward silence with each other.

"Well, I guess I better get going," she says.

"Yeah, do you need any help or anything?" Ken offers.

"No, I'm good. I guess this is goodbye," she replies.

"Yeah, I guess it is," Ken responds with sadness in his eyes.

Sharon notices his mood, goes into her book bag, and pulls out a notebook and a pen. She writes something on the paper, rips the page out of the notebook, and folds it before handing it to Ken.

"Something to remember me by," she says before hugging Ken.

Although the hug was a brief one, it meant the world to Ken. After a few moments, the two look at each other, still feeling a little awkward. Ken finally fights his fears as he tries to express himself.

"Sharon, I... look, I know that I have been... I guess I

just want to…" Ken stutters.

"I know," Sharon says, saving him. "I feel the same way. I guess we'll never know, right?"

Ken nods his head as Sharon smiles before collecting her things and walking down the hallway and out of the exit. After she's gone, Ken opens the note she had given him. It is a drawing of a heart inside of a box, with a line going down the middle of it. While he didn't know what the meaning of the symbol meant to her, he knew what it would mean to him. It would always be a reminder of lost love and how he should never live with regret. He sighs before folding the note back up and putting it in his pocket. After he ponders for a few moments, he finally makes his way down the hall and out of the school.

Chapter 2

My First (Paula Abdul – Rush Rush) - 1991

Summertime vacation is a few weeks away from ending. A now thirteen-year-old, Ken is sitting on the stoop in front of his home with his sunglasses on, enjoying his lazy summer. He looks across the street and sighs as he notices a new family had moved in across the street where his friend William used to live. Outside of Gilbert, William was one of his closest friends, so to see that his old friend was gone saddened him.

As he continues to look around the community from his stoop, he notices a young female walking from William's old front door. He lowers his glasses to check her out. She reminded him a little of Sharon with her blonde hair, but hers was longer and curlier. He's immediately drawn to her watching her walking to the mailbox in her shorts, flip flops, and a short shirt.

As she reaches her mailbox, she notices Ken sitting on the stoop looking at her. She smiles at him revealing her braces, which kills the mood for a moment. Ken has never been fond of girls with braces. He knew one from his class last year that would annoy the hell out of him. It's definitely not something he was looking for in any girl.

Ken smiles back at the female and nods. She quickly starts making her way towards him, catching him off guard. He's nervous as always as he quickly straightens himself out.

"Hey," the mysterious female says.

"Hey," a timid Ken responds.

"I'm Hilary. Just moved in across the street," she says with a smile.

"Yeah, I saw," Ken replies. "My friend used to live over there before his dad received new orders. He's in Georgia now. I was just thinking about all the times I used to hang out over there."

"Really?" Hilary responds with a smirk. "So, you've already been in my bedroom. That's kinda cool."

Ken chuckles as Hilary takes a seat next to him.

"So, you have a name, or am I gonna have to give you one?" she asks.

"Sorry, I'm Ken."

"Ken. Cute name," Hilary responds flirtatiously.

"Cute name? Never heard of my name being cute before," Ken replies.

"Really? I mean, with a name like Ken, I'm sure you have plenty of Barbies to choose from," Hilary responds with a smirk. "So, Ken, what do you do around here?"

"What do you mean?"

"Hello, for fun? I've been here a couple of days now, and I haven't seen a single thing cool to do around this place," she clarifies. "I mean, this place seems like a drag compared to where I come from."

"And where is it that you come from?" Ken asks, finally loosening up a bit.

"Well, I was living off base, but before that, I was at Fort Bragg," she answers as she leans back on the stoop.

"Heard it's nice out there," Ken says, still checking out his new friend.

"It's much better than this," she says. "I mean, I've been bored out of my mind since getting here. Could have just stayed off base."

Ken chuckles as Hilary smiles at him.

"Well, you just need to know who to talk to and all. You'll meet some new friends once school starts, and you'll be on your way. Trust me, it's not as dull as it looks here."

"Oh, I'm not gonna go to school here," Hilary informs. "At least not any time soon. My folks want me to stay at the school I'm going to off base. I think it's better or something. I don't know. I think I'd rather do that too. I like my friends there."

Ken nods his head with understanding. To have a girl who doesn't know him and his status at school is a plus.

"Well, tell you what, how about I introduce you around to a few people I know. I know summer is almost over, but at least when you are on base, you'll have a few friends to hang out with," he suggests.

"That would be so cool," an enthusiastic Hilary says. "So, you must be like the big man out here or something?"

"No, I'm nowhere close to being the big man," Ken admits. "I know a few people though. Enough to entertain you, I hope."

Hilary nods her head with a smile before checking her

watch. She slowly rises from the stoop, which gives Ken a full view of her legs.

"Well, let me get back to the house. I'll see you later then?" Hilary asks.

Ken nods before Hilary winks at him and hurries off. She checks the mailbox quickly and waves to Ken before rushing into her front door. Ken leans back on his stoop as if he's the man, feeling himself with a smirk on his face after his latest interaction with the opposite sex.

Later that night, Ken is lying in his room talking on the cordless phone to Gilbert, still excited with his earlier interaction.

"You're such a liar," Gilbert says, doubting his friend. "I don't buy it."

"Why would I make this up?" Ken asks.

"The same reason I made up having a girlfriend at another school," Gilbert responds. "To seem like you're finally talking to a girl."

"Dude, whatever!" Ken snaps back. "I don't make up stuff. She's cute too. She has braces, but I don't-"

"Braces?! No way, dude," Gilbert blurts out. "Are you crazy? Braces make girls weird. Never mess with any girl with braces."

Ken looks on confused.

"Wait a minute, didn't Brianna have braces?" he asks.

"Exactly! That's why I'm trying to warn you," Gilbert responds. "Metal does not belong in someone's mouth. Once it's there, all things start to go wild, trust me. Brianna didn't have braces when we first started going together, but a couple of weeks later, she showed up with the wire in her mouth and went crazy from there."

Ken ponders his friend's words before moving the conversation along.

"Anyway, you feel like meeting up this weekend? Heard Steve and a few folks are trying to get a water fight going," he says.

"Oh, so you want me to bring to super soaker, right?" a cocky Gilbert says.

"Well, duh! I mean, you are the only one who has one. Me and you teaming up, they don't stand a chance," Ken replies.

"Dude, please. I could take on all of you with the soaker," Gilbert gloats. "You need me. So don't think it has anything to do with you."

Ken grabs his head with frustration as Gilbert continues to go on and on. Before he can respond, he notices the light coming on from his old friend's William's bedroom. He rises from the bed, looks out of his window, and sees Hilary peering out of the window looking around the area. She notices him looking out of the window and smiles at him before waving. Ken waves back at her as she motions for him to meet her outside. He thinks for a minute before nodding his head with agreement.

Gilbert is still talking about his super soaker's superiority over everyone else when Ken quickly chimes in.

"Hey, I gotta go. Bye," he says, hanging up the phone and rushing downstairs.

He quickly makes his way into the kitchen and over to the garbage can. His mother is by the stove cooking dinner when he notices the can is half-empty. It doesn't matter to him, and he grabs the bag and ties the strings together. His mother looks at him strangely.

"Ken, what are you doing?" She inquires.

"Taking out the garbage," Ken replies as he lifts the bag out of the garbage can.

"That bag doesn't seem full enough for you to-"

His mother's words are ignored as he quickly runs out into the back yard with the bag before his mother can finish her statement. She shakes her head, writing off her son's erratic behavior to puberty before going back to cooking dinner.

Ken comes running from behind his building and meets up with Hilary, who is standing in her front yard. Ken is out of breath as he takes a moment to gather himself before speaking.

"Hey," he says while panting.

"Did you run all the way from your back yard?" Hilary asks with a smirk.

"Yes, had to take out the garbage and… you know what, never mind. Doesn't matter," he answers as he finally calming down. "What's up?"

"Nothing much. I was just checking out the view when I saw you. Were you on the phone with your girlfriend?" a curious Hilary asks.

"Huh? Girlfriend? I don't have a girlfriend," Ken replies. "Why? Do you have a boyfriend?"

"Have three actually," Hilary says with a smirk.

"Three boyfriends?"

"Yep."

"Why would you need three boyfriends?" Ken asks.

"Well, I have two back at Ft. Bragg. One's off base, and one's on base, and technically, I have one off base here, but he's probably moving, so I don't know."

Ken looks at Hilary with disappointment in his eyes before she bursts into laughter.

"I can't believe you fell for that," she says while laughing. "I don't have a boyfriend. My dad would kill me if I did. Not allowed to have one officially till I'm sixteen at the earliest, so I'm three years away."

Ken perks back up as Hilary laughs again.

"So does that make you happy?" she asks.

"A little. Why'd you call me down here?" a curious

Ken asks.

"To see if you would come," Hilary replies with a smirk. "And here you are."

Both teens stand silently as Ken looks around nervously.

"So, are you gonna ask me for my number?" Hilary inquires.

"Huh? Oh, well, I... I mean sure. What's your number?" Ken nervously asks.

"You can't have it," Hilary replies, disappointing Ken. "I can take yours though."

Ken's spirit picks back up as Hilary goes into her shorts and pulls out a paper and pen. He writes down his number and hands it back to her as she checks it out with a smile.

"I'm about to call you right now, so if I were you, I'd get running," she says before turning her back and walking into her home.

Ken rolls his eyes as he quickly runs around the building once more back into his back yard.

In his house, in the kitchen, the phone suddenly rings.

Ken's mother notices the phone on the table where he had left it before taking the garbage out. She's about to answer it when Ken flies in from the back yard and snatches the phone from the table before she's able to answer.

"It's for me!" he says before whizzing upstairs and back into his room.

His mother shakes her head, wondering if puberty going to make her son's behavior worse.

Ken plops down on the bed and gathers himself before finally answering the phone.

"Hello?"

"Hey. Didn't think you'd make it back in time," Hilary says.

"I'm one of the fastest guys at my school," Ken replies, trying to hide the fact that he's trying to catch his breath.

The two continue their conversation with Ken occasionally laughing as the two teens learn about each other, working to build a connection.

A couple of days later, Ken and Hilary are walking together before taking a seat at an unoccupied bench next to the playground. They both look over towards Ken's sister, Jermaia, who is playing with her friends on the monkey bars. Hilary is laughing as she scoots a little closer to Ken, making him a little anxious.

"Why do you always seem nervous?" she says, noticing how tense Ken was.

"I'm not nervous, I'm just… I don't know," he replies, unable to come up with an excuse.

"You just always seem a little jumpy when I get close," Hilary points out. "Have you ever had a girlfriend?"

Ken ponders a moment, thinking back to his thirty-second relationship with Sharon. It wasn't much, but in his eyes, it still counted.

"Yeah, I've had a girlfriend," he replies to Hilary, who isn't convinced.

"Yeah, that answer doesn't sound made up," she replies sarcastically.

"I'm serious. I did. It didn't last very long, but I did have one," Ken replies.

"Just the one?"

Ken nods his hand as Hilary chuckles to herself.

"Well, you're still new to it all. Don't worry, it gets easier. Trust me," she says. "Why did y'all break up?"

"Her dad was stationed in Colorado," Ken answers, trying to hide the fact that Sharon choosing Tim was the real reason for their short-lived relationship.

Hilary can tell that his past relationship was a touchy subject and decides to move on.

"The DYA was cool," she says with a smile. "You act like you're not the big man, but everybody there knew you."

"Not everybody, but I've been here for four years. Well, three years on base. My dad was in Korea, which is why we've been here so long. Most folks don't get to stay in one place like that," Ken says to an understanding, Hilary.

"Life of the army brat," she says with a smirk. "Last time I went home, I mean my real home in Nebraska, all the people from a long time ago are still there, just older. To grow up around the same people would be so cool. Anything is better than getting close with people, and having to move."

"Tell me about it," Ken says, understanding all too well the life on an army brat.

"Look at us, sharing a moment," Hilary says with a smile. "I like that."

"Me too."

"So, what are you doing tomorrow?" Hilary asks. "I wanna do that so-called dangerous bike trail you're always talking about."

Ken looks at her as if he's offended.

"So-called?" he quips. "I'm talking about crossing several back streets, through parking lots, all the way down to the main road. It's not for scary folks."

Hilary looks as though as if she's not impressed.

"I'll have my bike waiting," she says. "So it's a date?"

"It's a da-" Ken says before stopping in his tracks. "Damn, I forgot. I can't tomorrow. I'm hooking up with some folks for a water fight. Maybe the last big fight before school starts."

Hilary sighs as she rolls her eyes.

"You boys and your toys," she responds.

"Hey, you girls have your Barbie dolls, or whatever it

is you have, and we have our street battles. It's the way of the world," Ken replies with a smirk.

"So what. Cancel it. Come hang with me tomorrow," Hilary says to Ken, who looks at her as if he's offended.

"You must not understand how important these water fights are," Ken replies. "We have two, maybe three of these a summer if we're lucky. Everyone gets together and leave the streets dripping with the splatters of our victims. It's pretty intense."

Hilary rolls her eyes with Ken's animated explanation.

"I just don't see what the big deal is," she says with an attitude.

"Well, you wouldn't. You haven't been here that long. Besides, you wouldn't make it in the water fight world," Ken responds.

"Oh, I wouldn't?"

"Nope. This is where the real adults stand up. Not for the weak," Ken says with a smirk.

Hilary rolls her eyes once more as Ken's words start to get to her.

"What time is this big fight going on?" She asks.

"Around three at the park."

"Okay, great. That means tomorrow around eleven, me and you have a score to settle," Hilary says, confusing Ken. "Tomorrow, me and you battle. If I win the battle, you have to add me to your team tomorrow and the big fight. If you win, I owe you a kiss."

Ken bursts into laughter as he's shocked by his friend's offer.

"Battle? Me? In a water fight?" He responds with a confident smirk. "You don't want to go down that path, trust me."

"Sounds like you're chicken," Hilary responds, goading Ken.

"I'm not scared!" Ken fires back. "I could take on you on no problem. I'll even throw my sister in on your team."

"Then it's a bet?" Hilary asks, holding out her pinky to seal the deal.

Ken hesitates for a moment before pinky swearing Hilary to seal the bet.

"You're going to be sorry you made that bet," he says with a grin.

"We will see," she says as she stands up from the bench. "I have to go set up for tomorrow, but I'll see you out here at eleven. Send your sister out back around ten forty-five. I'll take it from there."

Ken nods his head in agreement. Hilary blows him a kiss before running off. He was ecstatic with the bet knowing once he won, he would have his first ever kiss. There was no way he'd lose to her in his head, even with his sister on her side.

"Jermaia! Come here," Ken says, calling out to his sister.

Jermaia runs over as he looks at her with a smile.

"How would you like to help my friend in a water fight?" He says with a sinister grin on his face.

The next morning, the playground was calm and silent, with a slight breeze in the air. Ken, who was equipped with a water gun and a book bag filled with water balloons, stealthily makes his way around the area. He leaves water balloons in strategic places, prepping for his battle. He makes his way behind some bushes and gets a good look at Hilary's back yard. He watches as his sister and Hilary look over the fence, waiting for his assault.

He smiles as he checks his water gun and balloon stash. He planned to lure Hilary out of the back yard towards the various balloon stashes he set up in the park. He's about to advance and put his plan in motion when he suddenly notices Gilbert walking down the sidewalk adjacent to Hilary's back yard, carrying his super soaker gun. Gilbert also notices him and smiles while waving.

"Yo, Ken!" He yells, giving away Ken's position.

Hilary smiles as she notices her friend as well. Ken reacts by running from behind the bush, trying to warn Gilbert to stay back.

"Gilbert! No! Don't move!" He yells back, trying to warn his friend.

The warning is too late as the sky fills with water balloons heading their way.

"Incoming!" Ken yells.

He's able to avoid the onslaught of balloons, but Gilbert isn't as fortunate, and he's drenched by multiple balloons at once. Ken offers cover fire as he grabs his friend pulling him to safety. Once behind the bushes, Gilbert looks around as if he's shell-shocked.

"What the hell was that?!" Gilbert asks.

"The girl I told you about! Me and her are in a water fight right now," Ken answers.

"Holy shit, she's real?!" A stunned Gilbert responds.

"Real, and on the offensive," Ken replies. "What are you doing here anyway?"

"I came over to see what the plan was for three," Gilbert responds. "I didn't know I would walk into World War three here!"

"Well, you're here now, and you're a part of it! They've struck first, so you know that that means," Ken says to his friend, who nods his head with understanding.

"It means war is upon us," Gilbert replies as he starts pumping his super soaker. "Wait 'til they get a load of me."

Ken nods his head, noticing Hilary and Jermaia have left her stronghold to hid behind nearby bushes looking to attack once again.

"Aim for the bushes," Ken says before he breaks cover and throws a barrage of balloons toward the bushes Hilary and his sister were kidding behind.

Gilbert also fires his super soaker as well, drenching them both as they run to the far corner of the playground. Ken runs over to his hidden stash of balloons in the area and continues his assault on the girls. Hilary is confused until she noticed Ken was getting support from Gilbert. After taking heavy water, Hilary pulls at Jermaia as the two retreat. Ken chases them as he's switched to his water gun, taunting Hilary.

"Why are you running? What are you scared of?" He mocks.

Hilary and Jermaia make it to the safety of her back yard and slams the gate shut. Gilbert runs over and joins Ken just outside the gate. Ken gives him several more balloons from his bookbag with a smirk on his face.

"Make this easy and open up!" Ken yells, calling Hilary out.

"Nope! You want it, come get it! Hilary yells back.

The gate is wooded, and visibility is limited. Gilbert looks towards Ken, looking for answers.

"So, what now?" He asks.

"I say we go. She's not ready for us," Ken says. "Besides, it's us versus them, and my nine-year-old sister is on her team."

"You sure about this?"

Ken smiles and he nods his head.

"Let's rock," he says as he quickly opens the latch to the gate.

Both Ken and Gilbert rush in but are surprised when they notice Jermaia is armed with the yard hose pointing at them, and Hilary is holding a super soaker, a newer model than what Gilbert had.

"Aw poo," Gilbert says before both he and Ken are attacked.

Hilary has a sadistic smile as she drenches Ken, who is trying to retreat but can't open the latch thanks to Hilary's attack. The attack pushes them into the far corner of the yard with no way out. Ken throws several balloons towards Hilary that hit their mark, enraging her. She hands Jermaia her super soaker and takes control of the hose. She makes sure she sprays Ken well, as both he and Gilbert slip onto the ground, exposed and out of ammo.

"Okay! Okay! I give up! I give up!" Ken yells.

Hilary is relentless, and she continues to drench Ken for several more moments before finally letting up. She and Jermaia celebrate their victory as Ken and Gilbert lay on the ground in shame.

"Hey, what's the name of that movie they made us watch in history class last year?' Gilbert asks. "You know the one with the Civil War?"

"Glory?" Ken responds.

"Yeah, that one. Remember the end of that movie? I finally understand the ending of it," Gilbert responds as he rolls over to the side.

Ken looks over towards Hilary, who smiles at him, knowing she got the best of him that day.

Later that evening, after the great playground water war of the summer, Ken is sitting on a bench soaking wet, trying to dry himself off. Hilary returns holding her boom box, a couple of towels, and her book bag. She tosses a towel over to Ken before turning on her boom box to play the radio.

"Thanks," Ken says as he starts to dry himself off.

"I'm not gonna lie, that was fun," Hilary says with a smile as she takes a seat next to Ken and starts to dry off herself.

"Yeah. They weren't ready for you," Ken admits. "Glad you were on my team."

"Yeah. I had to teach you a lesson to get on your team, but I'm glad I was on your team too," Hilary admits while bobbing her head to the music playing.

Ken tosses the towel to the side and looks around the area as the sun has just set.

"Nice out tonight," he says as Hilary nods her head in agreement.

"Yeah, it really is," she responds before Paula Abdul's *Rush Rush* starts playing on the radio. "Oh my God! I love this song! This has to be our song!"

Ken is confused as Hilary closes her eyes and begins sway.

"Our song?" He asks.

"Yeah. You know how couples have a song and stuff. This should be our song," she replies.

Ken is stunned as Hilary continues to sway.

"So... So we're a couple now?" Ken inquires as Hilary opens her eyes with a smirk.

"Sure. Just don't tell my dad," she says as she digs into her book sack. "Once your name is in the songbook, we are official."

She takes out a book labeled songbook from her bag and opens it up. She writes down Ken's name and the song Rush Rush next to it. Ken looks on curiously, still stunned that he's in a relationship. If it lasted after the song finished playing, it would be the longest relationship he's ever been in.

"Songbook? What's that about?" He asks.

Hilary smiles as she places her book back into her bag.

"Music is what defines us," she explains. "Music is how I experience life and how I remember special events and people. You do too, but you just don't track it. I'll prove it to you. Your last girlfriend, what was her name?"

"Um... Sharon?" A confused Ken responds.

"Sharon? What an odd name," Hilary says before moving on. "Anyway, what's a song that makes you think about her? You could be riding in the car, or watching TV, and this song comes on, and it immediately makes you think about her."

This was an easy answer for Ken as the dance where he watched Sharon dancing with Tim will always haunt him.

"New Kids on the Block, Please Don't Go, Girl," Ken answers. "But not for a good reason, trust me."

"It doesn't matter," Hilary points out. "Good or bad, music is life. It may make you sad when you hear it, but it brings you to a place that things like pictures can't. I want you to start a songbook, and my name better be in there with Paula Abdul as our song."

Ken chuckles while shaking his head.

"Sounds crazy if you ask me," he replies.

"Trust me, you'll thank me later," she quips. "Anything that you go through, or any relationship you're in, write it down. Every time you hear our song in the future, no matter what happens, you'll always think about me just like I'll always think about you when I hear it."

Ken thinks for a few moments before nodding his head

in agreement.

"Alright, I think I can do that. I mean, since we're a couple and all now, I guess I can try it out," Ken responds, causing his new girlfriend to smile.

Hilary continues to enjoy the music as an excited Ken smiles, knowing that he has his first ever real girlfriend. He finally can let go of the Sharon fiasco from earlier that year. He cautiously looks around to make sure that Tim or any other classmate wasn't lurking in the bushes looking to take his spot once again.

"Hey, next weekend, there's not a massive water fight, or something crazy going on, is there?" Hilary asks.

"Nah, nothing that I can think of," he responds.

"Cool. My friend Veronica is coming to stay over next weekend. Is it cool she hangs with us?" Hilary asks.

"Cool with me," Ken replies.

"Rad. Hey, can you set her up with one of your friends?" Hilary requests. "I mean, it would be more fun if she had a guy of her own while she's visiting."

Ken nods his head much to the delight of his new girlfriend. She lays her head on his shoulder as the two enjoy each other's company listening to music.

Later that night, Ken walks into his bedroom, goes into his closet, and pulls out an empty notebook and pen. He lays down on his bed as he opens the book to the first page. He writes down Sharon's name first, and her song before doing the same for Hilary. He closes the book and writes 'My Song Book' on the front of it just before Jermaia barges into his room, upsetting him.

"Didn't they teach you how to knock?!" He snaps.

"Sorry, you have a phone call, but if you don't want it…" Jermaia replies before starting to walk out.

"Wait!" Says Ken before jumping out of bed and grabbing the phone from his little sister.

As she walks out, he closes the door behind her and plops back down to his bed.

"Hello," he answers.

It's Gilbert on the line, which brings a smile to his face.

"Gil, my main man," he says with a hint on arrogance in his voice. "Guess who now has a girlfriend, and guess who's going to hook you up as well?"

Ken laughs as he talks to his friend about his new relationship and other events that went on throughout the day.

Several days later, Ken is watching his father hook up a cable box to their downstairs television. His mother and Jermaia are also watching as his father turns to them before turning on the TV.

"Okay, so this box has what they call a chip in there," his father explains to them. "What that means is we get all the cable channels now. Now the only reason I got this is because I want to see all of the movie channels. It does have these adult channels on here, and I need the two of you to steer clear of those channels. They are channels ninety-eight, and ninety-nine. Do you two understand?"

Both Ken and Jermaia nod their heads with understanding before their father turns on the TV. Everyone is excited about the new channels as the family gathers to enjoy their new stations.

Late Thursday night, Ken and Gilbert are in the living

room watching one the forbidden porn channels stunned at what they're watching. Both are silent with their mouths wide open with the volume down low, hoping to avoid detection.

"Is this what sex is?" Gilbert asks, cringing as he watches the TV.

"No way our parents did this," Ken chimed in. "I mean, it doesn't even make any sense."

"What I'm trying to understand is why is the girl sucking on the guy's thing?" Gilbert points out. "I mean, that's nasty!"

"Probably so she doesn't get pregnant," Ken replies.

"You said that when we were watching the video of the guy sticking his thing in the girl's booty hole earlier," Gilbert points out. "Do you even know what you're talking about?"

"No! That's why we're watching this, dummy," Ken quips. "We have to know how to do this someday or it's the end of the human race."

The two are silent as one sexual act stuns them.

"Turn it off, turn it off, turn it off!" Gilbert exclaims as

Ken struggles with the remote and changes the channel to a friendlier station.

Both are relieved as Ken grabs his head in frustration.

"I don't know if I could do any of that," he says.

"I don't know how anyone does any of that," quips Gilbert. "No wonder folks say just say no."

"That's for drugs, Gil," Ken points out. "I just hope she doesn't have Aids, 'cause I don't want that."

Gilbert looks at Ken strangely after his last comment.

"Oh my God," he says, figuring his friend out. "You think we're gonna have to do this tomorrow?!"

"No! Well, I don't know. Maybe?" a conflicted Ken responded.

"Are you out of your mind?" Gilbert responds. "I'm not doing this, and you shouldn't either!"

"Why not?"

"Because I'm not trying to be like Khondo!"

Ken is confused with Gilbert bringing up one of his classmates.

"Khondo? What about him?" he asks.

Gilbert sighs before going on with his story.

"You remember Jamila from the eighth grade? The one who left early last year?" Gilbert asks.

"Yeah."

"Do you know why she left earlier?" He asks Ken, who responds with a shrug.

"Her and Khondo had sex, and she ended up pregnant," Gilbert reveals, stunning his friend. "She had to go to another school because of it. I mean, Khondo is still with us, but he's gonna be a father sometime soon if he isn't already. Do you know what that means?"

"Yeah. It means we should have asked him about sex instead of watching the nasty stuff we just did," Ken responds, causing Gilbert to grab his head.

"No, you idiot! It means his life is over," Gilbert answers. "No more games, hanging out, or anything like that. He has a child to take care of now. Think about how that feels."

Ken thinks for several moments. He hadn't thought much about the possible repercussions of having sex with Hilary. He wasn't even sure if he wanted to have sex, just believing that's what couples do.

"I guess I never thought about that," he says.

"I know you haven't. That's why I'm here." Gilbert says with a smirk. "You're still on your first girlfriend. I'm on my third, going on my fourth if things work out tomorrow. I'm experienced."

Ken looks at his friend strangely.

"Okay, last I checked, you've had two official girlfriends," Ken points out. "That made up one that went to a different school doesn't count. Technically, I have more of a claim since me and Sharon were together for about thirty seconds. So we're about even."

"I did have a girlfriend that went to another school," Gilbert fires back. "She was over by my house that one time you were sick. I called you and everything to come meet her."

Both Ken and Gilbert go back and forth with each other trying to argue the validity of Gilbert's other school girlfriend, and Ken's Sharon claim. The discussion deflects Ken's concern about having sex for the moment, but in the back of his mind, he knew he'd have to make that choice one day.

The next evening, Ken and Gilbert are in Ken's front yard tossing the football back and forth, waiting for their dates for the evening. Ken keeps looking towards Hilary's home across the street as Gilbert approaches him after one final pass.

"So what time did they say they were gonna meet us?" Gilbert asks.

"She didn't say," Ken answers.

"Damn, man. I don't know if I can stay much longer. My mom wants me in early tonight cause we're leaving out first thing in the morning," Gilbert explains. "She only let me stay over last night if I promised to be in early today."

"Relax, dude. They'll be here," Ken reassures even though he's feeling a little skeptical himself.

"Yeah, well, she better not be ugly, Ken. Having me waste my time," Gilbert responds.

Ken shakes his head when he notices Hilary and her friend Veronica walking out of her front door. He smirks as he turns Gilbert's attention towards them.

"Yeah, she's really ugly," a sarcastic Ken responds as he and his friend both check out Veronica.

She immediately catches Gilbert's attention with her flowing dark hair and hazel eyes. She's cute and actually looks better than Hilary in Ken's opinion. Both friends are dressed in shorts and flip flops as they approach Ken and Gilbert.

"Hey," Hilary says as she shares a quick hug with Ken.

"Hey," he responds.

"Hey, so this is my friend Veronica from off post. Ronnie, this is my boyfriend Ken, and his friend... Gilbert, right?" Hilary says, introducing everyone to Veronica.

"Yeah, that's me," a confident Gilbert says with a smile on his face.

Veronica looks him over, forces a smile on her face, and waves to Gilbert before taking a look at Ken.

"So, you're the boyfriend Hil keeps talking about?" Veronica says with a smirk.

"Oh, so she's talking about me?" Ken replies with a grin. "What's she saying about me?"

"Only that you're so cute, and all that. She's right," Veronica responds, embarrassing Hilary, who turns red.

"That's enough, big mouth," she replies as she walks

over to Ken and grasps his hand. "Go play with Gilbert while me and my boyfriend have some us time."

Veronica rolls her eyes as she grabs Gilbert by his arm and walks off, much to his delight. Hilary shakes her head as she and Ken take a seat on his stoop. Ken watches Gilbert and Veronica's interaction and smiles at an excited Gilbert.

"Cute friend," he says to Hilary. "Looks like Gilbert really likes her.

"Well, she doesn't seem to share the same feelings," Hilary responds, watching Veronica look seemingly bored.

"She'll warm up to him. Maybe she's just a little nervous," Ken responds.

"You don't know Veronica, trust me," Hilary replies with a smirk. "Anyway, enough about them. How you've been doing?"

Ken smiles as he and Hilary continue their conversation catching up with each other.

Thirty minutes later, Hilary and Ken are returning from their brief walk around the building when they notice

Veronica sitting on Hilary's stoop looking for them. Hilary leads Ken across the street towards her house.

"Hey, Ronnie, what's up? Where's Gilbert?" Hilary asks her friend.

"He had to leave. Said he needed to do something or another in the morning," Veronica answers.

"Yeah, he's going out of town," Ken clarifies.

"Not far enough," Veronica comments, causing Ken to shake his head.

"So, I take it that didn't go so well?" Ken says as he and Hilary take a seat next to Veronica.

"Don't get me wrong, he's a cool guy and all, it's just… well, he's really not my type, that's all," Veronica replies.

"Okay, I can understand that," Ken says, nodding his head.

"Yeah, it's cool, Ronnie. I'm sure Ken can set you up with someone else," Hilary says while looking at Ken.

"Oh, yeah, I can," Ken replies. "I think you'll like my friend Steve. He lives down the block. I can give him a call and see if he can come over. He doesn't have a girlfriend or anything as far as I know, and I think he'd be-"

"Is he black?" Veronica replies, cutting off Ken.

Ken is stunned and is confused with Veronica's response.

"Huh?"

"Is he black?"

"Well… no, he's white," Ken answers, still stunned with Veronica's request.

Veronica gives Hilary a look, as Hilary nods her head looking to clarify Veronica's request.

"Look, Ken, we were hoping for a black guy to get with Ronnie," Hilary says.

"I don't understand, why does he have to be black?" Ken asks.

"I don't know, it's just… I guess you could say black guys are our type, you know. It's just what we like, that's all" Hilary answers.

Ken sighs as Veronica awaits his answer.

"I… well damn… I guess I can think about who I know that lives in the area that I can bring over," Ken says, still flabbergasted with what he's hearing. "I'll see what I can do."

"Thanks, babe! You're the greatest," Hilary says with a smile.

Ken forces a smile on his face as he nods his head in agreement.

"Well, since it seems my friend is dateless tonight, I guess I'm going to go ahead and head in," Hilary says, rising from the stoop. "Call me if you get someone over tonight, and we can come back out and hang, cool?"

Ken rises from the stoop and nods his head.

"Sure, I guess," he replied.

Hilary gives Ken a quick hug before she and Veronica walk into her house, giggling with each other. Ken slowly walks back towards his home in deep thought, trying to figure out what just happened. Several thoughts raced through his mind as he never thought about things like race when dealing with someone. He started to wonder if Hilary only liked him because he was black. None of what just happened felt right to him. As he makes it to his stoop, he takes one last look at Hilary's home before walking into his front door.

The next day, Ken is lying on his bed looking at his football card collection book, when his sister Jermaia walks into his room with the cordless phone in her hand.

"Hey, Hilary is on the phone," she says as she tosses the phone to her brother much to his displeasure.

After she's gone, Ken takes a deep breath before answering the phone.

"Hey... Oh no... I... I just don't feel good today," Ken says, trying to avoid seeing her and Veronica. "Yeah... I think it was something I ate... I know... no, it's cool. I'll take to you when I feel better...okay... bye."

Ken hangs up the phone and tosses it on the side of the bed. He didn't want to see Hilary as long as Veronica was around. He hoped that once the two were alone together that things would become as they were before all the unexplained racial tension came about. He still was unsure about her thoughts towards him, and he'd rather not deal with it for the moments.

Two weeks later, Ken is at the local basketball court hooping with Gilbert and several others. They were playing on the modified hoop, which was shortened for younger kids so that they can dunk and play basketball like their NBA idols. Ken is having a monster game since he was taller than most of the group as he slams down a devastating dunk on his peers. He laughs, feeling unstoppable when he suddenly notices Hilary standing courtside observing him. The smile drops from his face as he turns to the others in the group.

"Time out," he says, much to their displeasure as he jogs over to meet with his girlfriend.

"Hey, what are you doing here?" he asks Hilary.

"Looking for you," she responds. "It's been almost two weeks now, and I haven't seen or heard from you. The only reason I knew you were here is because your sister told me when I stopped by your house."

Ken shakes his head, thinking about how his sister runs her mouth too much.

"Yeah, I know. I've been so busy as of late," Ken says. "I'm sorry, I should have called."

"Ken, Summer is almost over. I'm going back off post in a few days to get ready for school. How could you waste the little time we had?" a saddened Hilary asks, looking for answers.

"I know and I'm sorry. I've just been busy, that's all," Ken says, trying to calm Hilary down.

"You're supposed to be my boyfriend!" Hilary exclaims, getting a little too loud for Ken's comfort.

"Look, can we talk about this later?" Ken responds.

"How about we talk about it now?" Hilary questions.

Before Ken can respond, one of the players on the court calls out to him.

"Yo, Ken, we gonna do this or what?" he says, referring to continuing the game.

Ken thinks for a moment before answering.

"Alright, I'll be there in a sec," he says before turning his attention to Hilary.

"Look, I'll stop by when I get done here. Cool?" he says to her.

Hilary shakes her head as a few tears fall from her face.

"You know what? Don't bother," she responds before storming off.

Ken is about to reach out to her but notices all of his

friends looking his way. He sighs before joining his friends back on the court to continue their game.

Later that night, Ken is in his room with the cordless phone dialing Hilary's number. There is no answer on the line as Ken looks outside his window and notices her bedroom light is on. Knowing she's there, Ken tries to call once more before finally hanging up the line. He plops down on his bed feeling guilty with the way he treated Hilary. He realized that whatever it was that attracted her to him in the first place didn't matter. He liked her and missed hanging with her. His stubbornness cost him two weeks that he'll never get back.

A few days later, Ken was sitting out on his stoop tossing the football to himself, hoping to catch a glimpse of Hilary. He'd called her multiple times in the past few days, but she never answered. Her father did one time and told him to stop calling her since he kept ringing the line. After that, Ken decided it would be best to just wait to see if he could catch her outside of her home.

A car pulls up in the front of Hilary's house, and Ken is ecstatic when he notices Hilary walking outside of her front door. His mood is short-lived as he noticed that she was carrying a couple of duffle bags with her. Her father also exits the house with a couple of bags that they both load into the car. Hilary refused to look into Ken's direction as she helped load the car. After a few moments, her father talks to the driver, who seems like a family member, before Hilary gets into the front seat of the car.

After a few moments, the car starts up as Ken realizes that this is the last time he'd ever see Hilary. He sighs, begging for her to just make eye contact to acknowledge his presence. She doesn't give him the satisfaction as the car pulls off down the road, and turns on the corner. Ken is heartbroken with the way things left off with his first girlfriend. He still had his doubts if she likes him for him, or because he was black, but it didn't matter at that point. She was gone from his life, and they didn't even have a proper goodbye between them. A saddened Ken slowly makes his way into his house and up to his room. He walks over to his radio and loads his Paula Abdul CD he had purchased into it. He plays the song Rush Rush and plops down into his bed. His eyes were watered as Hilary was right when she says he would never be able to listen to that song without thinking about her. He rose from the bed and put the song on repeat. He wanted to remind himself of the fun times they had before it all went bad. He blamed himself for how things ended and wanted to torment himself with her memory.

Chapter 3

Eight Grade Arranged Marriages (Another Bad
Creation - Iesha) – 1991-92

It's just after the winter break as students have returned from Christmas, all wearing their new outfits and talking about their free time. Ken, now in eighth grade, walks into his Homeroom class and takes a seat at his desk. He's talking to his neighbor when Valarie, one of his other classmates, walks over and taps him on the shoulder, grabbing his attention.

"Hey, Ken," she says.

"Hey, Valarie. What's up?" Ken responds as he checks her out.

Valarie wasn't one of Ken's normal crew he dealt with. She was one of the elusive black females that stayed mostly with the popular kids. Her reaching out to Ken was strange, to say the least, but on the other hand, she is cute, and Ken doesn't mind entertaining anyone of her status.

"I got a question I wanna ask you," she responds as she has Ken's full attention.

"Sure," he replies with a smirk.

"So, you down with O.P.P.?" Valarie asks, confusing Ken.

"Am I down with what?"

"O.P.P.? You down with O.P.P.?" she repeats.

Ken is lost, as he has no clue what she's talking about. He thought maybe this was some joke Valarie was playing on him. Still, he needed a response. Is he said yes, and it's something that made him look stupid, it would ruin the rest of his eighth-grade year, and probably carry over to the ninth grade. If he said no, it may be something that made him look non-cool in the eyes of his eighth-grade peers. After careful thought, he decides to go with the latter as he wasn't particularly popular anyway, and admitting yes not knowing what it meant could have worse repercussions.

"Ummm, no?" Ken responds as if he's questioning her.

Valarie giggles as she looks back to the table where Iyesha, Shalona, and Latoya are sitting. They are the popular black girls in the eighth grade.

"I told y'all he wouldn't know," Valarie says as Iyesha approaches them.

"Leave dude alone," Iyesha told her friend. "You know he hangs with them white folks. He's not gonna know anything about that."

Ken is confused as Valarie giggles once more.

"Okay, what's the joke?" Ken asks. "What am I missing here?"

Iyesha nods to Valarie, who gets herself together.

"You're supposed to say, 'Yeah, you know me,'" Valarie responds.

"Why?" Ken asks.

"O.P.P. Stands for Other People's Property," Valarie explains. So, when someone asks, you down with O.P.P., you respond, 'yeah, you know me.'

Ken is still confused about the discussion.

"Other people's property?" he asks. "Why would I be down with other people's property?"

"I can't. I just can't," Valarie says before walking off and heading back to her section, leaving Iyesha and Ken alone.

Ken looks to Iyesha, searching for answers as she shakes her head with a smirk. Unlike Valarie, Iyesha was more friendly to those around her, even the ones not on the popularity level as she was. Ken dreamed once that he and she kissed as he's always had a crush on her. She was cute with the perfect face in his opinion. Unlike Valarie, who had a makeup filled face, Iyesha preferred to keep her face makeup-free. She had the perfect smile, and her body developed a lot faster than others in the class, making her one of the more shapely girls in eighth grade. She wore a lot of trendy clothes and was known for her black pride, supporting all things African American.

"It's a song, Ken," she explains. "Naughty by Nature. The rap group. You know who that is right?"

Ken shakes his head, stunning Iyesha.

"Damn, you really are gone, aren't you?" she says. "Do you even listen to rap?"

"I mean, I do, but I just never heard of Naughty Nature," Ken responds.

"Naughty by Nature," Iyesha corrects. "Who you listen to then?"

"I listen to Vanilla Ice and M.C. Hammer," Ken says proudly, causing Iyesha to cringe. "Oh, and the Fresh

Prince."

"Well, Fresh Prince is dope. I don't know about that Vanilla Ice and Hammer though," Iyesha responds with a smirk. "You need to enhance your music for real, and listen to the real rap out there."

"Like who?" Inquires Ken.

"Like N.W.A. and Ice Cube," Iyesha suggests. "Oh, and Black Sheep, and Public Enemy. Fresh Prince is cool, but he's not spittin' the knowledge like them groups."

"My dad has the Boyz in the Hood album. I've heard Ice Cube," Ken says, trying to maintain some sort of credibility.

"Really? So what you think?" Iyesha asks.

"I liked it. Thought it was really dope," Ken replies, using her terminology.

"That's cool. Get on that Naughty by Nature though, for real," Iyesha says to a nodding Ken.

"Maybe I will," Ken responds.

Iyesha smiles at Ken before making her way back towards her friend's table.

Five minutes later, homeroom is over as the bell rings.

Ken grabs his bag and walks out into the hallway. Gilbert, who is walking out of his homeroom class as well, meets him a little way down the hall.

"What's up, man?" Gilbert says as they walk towards Ken's locker.

"Nothing much," Ken says before stopping in his tracks and turning to his friend.

"Say, let me ask you something. Are you down with O.P.P.?" he asks.

Gilbert looks at him strangely confused by the questioning.

"Dude, what the hell are you talking about?" he asks his friend.

"Are you down with O.P.P.?" Ken repeats.

"I don't know what the hell O.P.P., QRT, or LMNOP is," a frustrated Gilbert says. "What's the matter with you?"

"Naughty by Nature, my friend," Ken says with a smile before going into his locker.

Gilbert is still confused as he watches Ken swaps out books from his locker.

A week later, Ken is sitting in his Home Economics class chatting with several folks around him, waiting for the class to start. After a few moments, Ms. Parker walks in the class and gets everyone's attention as the class calms down.

"Okay, everyone. Today is the day where I assign everybody their partners for our next project that will be fifty percent of your grade," she tells the class, grabbing their attention. "Now I'm sure everyone has heard about this project before, but this year we're going to change it up. This year I will pair each of you with a pretend spouse as you all will be married partners for the duration of the project."

There are slight chatters with the class amongst themselves. Ken, for one, was happy with the announcement. He sat right next to Corrina, a person he's been trying to speak with for the last several months. He believed she liked him as well but didn't know how to approach her. Since they sat next to each other, he thought it would be a forgone conclusion that he'd be partnered with her. As Ms. Parker called out names, Ken and the rest of the class are anxiously awaiting to see who they're partnered with. He's shocked when Corrina is partnered with Larry who sits in the back of the classroom.

His mood is short-lived, however, when it's announced he was paired up with Iyesha, who looks over to him with a smirk from across the room. While he was disappointed, Ken figured he could have done worse than Iyesha.

"Okay, now what I want you all to do is to relocate your seats next to our partner. I'll let you work out who moves where. Take ten minutes to get together," Ms. Parker instructs after assigning everyone their partner.

All the students rise from their chairs and collect their things as they began to relocate as instructed. Iyesha waves Ken over as she wasn't moving her seat, rather wanting Ken to move towards her. He collects his things and quickly relocates to her area, taking a seat in the desk next to her.

"Well then, seems like our grades are connected with each other," Iyesha says as Ken gets comfortable in his new chair.

"Seems that way," he responds.

"Look, I'm not gonna front. I'm used to gettin' A's in all my classes, so you better come correct on this project," she responds.

"Relax. I'm no dummy," Ken reminds her. "Maybe not straight A's like you, but I can hold my own."

Iyesha nods her head when she notices Ken taking glimpses of Corrina sitting with Larry in the back of the class.

"You was hoping to work with your girl back there weren't you?" she says with a smirk on her face.

"Huh? What are you talking about?" Ken inquires.

"I see you checkin' out Corrina," Iyesha replies. "My guess is you thought Ms. Parker was gonna put y'all together cause y'all sit next to each other. You don't understand how things work though."

Ken is confused, scratching his head trying to figure out what Iyesha is talking about.

"What do you mean how things work?" He asks.

"Look around class. Don't you see anything strange?" Iyesha says.

Ken quickly glances around the class but doesn't see

anything out of the ordinary in his eyes. He looks back towards his partner and shrugs as Iyesha rolls her eyes.

"There are three black people, and one Hispanic in class," Iyesha points out. "And we're all partnered with each other. I guess we should be happy that there are two girls and two boys between us. Probably wouldn't have mattered either way."

"Wait, so you're saying that we were partnered together cause we're black?" Ken questions.

"I mean, all the white students are partnered with their own. Shalona and Jesus are together, and we're together. You tell me how that wasn't done on purpose," Iyesha says.

Ken thinks for a minute as he glances over towards Shalona and Jesus who are laughing and joking with each other. He looks at the rest of the predominately white class and notices their interaction as well. It never occurred to him that race had anything to do with class. He looks back to Iyesha who smiles at him while nodding her head. He leans back in his chair still shocked by the reveal.

After class is over, all the students who were paired

together have been issued a flour sack baby that they are to care for and log. Iyesha and Ken are still sitting in class going over their plans.

"Okay, so I'll take her this week, you'll take her next week, and we'll alternate until the project is done," Iyesha says. "You cool with that?"

"Yeah, I'm good," Ken says.

"Now make sure you log everything cause we're gonna be graded on our notes. If you do anything like go outside or whatever, make sure your parents sign off watching her, and please don't forget to feed my baby," Iyesha says causing Ken to chuckle.

"You know this is just a sack of flour right?" Ken points out. "I mean, technically we could just put the damn thing in the closet and fill out the forms."

"You know the whole point of school is to learn, right?" Iyesha replies. "I mean, I'm sure most folks in here are gonna do just that. I don't wanna go that route. I actually wanna take this seriously. If you don't wanna do it, I'll just take her and do it myself."

Ken notices how serious Iyesha is with this project. She

was determined to follow the project as it's written. He sighs and nods his head in agreement.

"Fine, I'll do it the right way," Ken responds. "So, since you already said it's a she, what do we name her?"

Iyesha thinks for a moment trying to come up with the perfect name.

"Let's call her Angela. After Angela Davis," Iyesha suggests.

Ken nods his head in agreement, but Iyesha can tell he has no idea who Angela Davis is.

"She's a political activist," Iyesha points out. "Don't you know anything about your history?"

"I must have missed that day in class," Ken replies.

"You're not gonna learn that in school," Iyesha says as she rises from her chair and packs her things. "My parents make sure I know that type of stuff. We need to learn our history because these folks here sure not gonna teach it to us."

Ken rises from his seat as well as he gathers his things. Iyesha grabs her flour baby and walks out of the class, followed closely by Ken.

"You gotta get down with the culture, Ken," Iyesha says while walking down the hall. "Don't just settle for the knowledge they offer. Look for the truth in the world."

As Iyesha makes it to her locker, she's met by Chad, captain of the football team. The two share a hug as Ken looks on. For all of Iyesha's pro-black attitude, she didn't mind dating a white guy, which Ken looks on as hypocritical. He was the typical white guy with blonde hair and blue eyes. He had a strong muscular build and was the most popular athlete in school.

"Hey, Chad," Iyesha says with a giggle before introducing Ken. "Hey, let me introduce you to my husband, Ken. Ken, this is my boyfriend, Chad."

Chad looks at Iyesha with confusion for a moment before nodding his head with understanding.

"Oh, you're in Ms. Parker's class this semester, right," he says before acknowledging Ken with a head nod. "So, what's up with you? You want to go to the DYA and hang out?"

"Can't. Gotta take care of my baby," Iyesha says, pointing towards her flour sack. "Probably gonna be busy all week with this. Next week is Ken's week though, so we can hook up then."

Chad is disappointed initially but nods his head in agreement.

"Okay, next week it is then," he says before sharing a hug with her once more. "Alright, I'm out."

Chad walks off as Ken looks at Iyesha with a smirk on his face.

"What?" Iyesha asks when she notices Ken's smug look.

"Nothing. Nothing at all," Ken replies as he begins walking off.

"Hey, wait!" Iyesha shouts catching his attention. "I need your number just in case something comes up with the baby."

Ken looks at his partner strangely, as she's taking this parenthood thing way too seriously. He walks back over as the two exchange numbers with each other before going their separate ways.

A few weeks later, Ken is at the DYA playing

basketball with Gilbert and a few others before the group disbands and gives the court to another group who is waiting to play. Ken and Gilbert take a seat in an unoccupied booth trying to cool down.

"You see that," Ken boasts. "I was on fire out there!"

"Yeah, you got lucky," Gilbert responds, ignoring his friend's performance. "You're just taller than all of us."

"Well, that's what basketball is," Ken reminds his friend. "Don't get mad because I have the height, and you're just pudgy."

Gilbert shakes his head in denial when he suddenly notices Shalona and Valarie walk into the building.

"Looks like your wife's squad just walked in," Gilbert says, pointing them out to Ken. "So, how's the marriage to one of the popular girls working out?"

"It's cool, I guess," Ken responds. "I mean, she can be a hard ass at times, making sure I'm doing the whole baby thing right. And don't even mention balancing the checkbook assignment. She spends a fortune on clothes leaving me to buy my stuff from K-Mart and Payless. Said I'm not stylish, so I can get by with that. It's crazy for real."

Gilbert laughs at his friend's struggles.

"Damn, dude. It seems like you're married for real," Gilbert says with a chuckle.

"It feels that way I swear. I mean why should I shop at K-Mart?" Ken asks. "I hate that damn store. Supposed to meet her in a few to take Angela from her for the week."

"Who?"

"Angela. Our daughter," Ken says.

"Jeez, dude. Seems to me you're taking this a little serious yourself," Gilbert points out.

Ken chuckles when he notices Iyesha walking in the building. She's not her usual self as he can tell she's upset about something. Both Shalona and Valarie hug her as they walk over to a nearby corner.

"What's going on here?" Ken says bringing his friend's attention to the commotion that's going on at the other end.

"Looks like she's crying," Gilbert says as they continue to observe from a distance.

Ken looks on with concern when he notices Shalona walking over to the concession stand.

"I'm going to go check it out," he says to his friend

before hopping out of the booth and meeting up with Shalona.

"Hey, Shalona," Ken greets as he approaches her. "What's going on? Iyesha looks like she's upset."

"Hey. She broke up with Chad," Shalona responds, stunning Ken.

"Broke up? Why?" Ken asks.

"He was cheating on her with Rebecca," Shalona responds.

"Rebecca? The one with the good hair?" Ken asks.

"Yeah, that's the one. Jerk was mad 'cause Iyesha wouldn't go out with him one day when she was taking care of the flour kid. Her mother wouldn't watch her, so after she told him no, he went out with Rebecca," Shalona says as Ken nods his head with understanding.

"Wow, that's messed up," he replies as Shalona gets her drink from the worker.

"Fucked up is more like it," Shalona responds. "You should come over and show her some support."

"I don't know. Seems like her friends should be the ones to talk with her," Ken responds.

"Well, you're her friend, aren't you?" Shalona points out. "Come on, she needs your support too."

Before Ken can respond, Shalona grabs him by his arm and leads him over towards Iyesha and Valarie, who are all standing together. Shalona hands Iyesha the drink as Ken notices she's struggling with her emotions.

"Hey, I just heard what happened," Ken says. "I'm sorry."

"Yeah, well. Lesson learned," Iyesha says as she wipes tears from her face. "Look, I'm gonna head out. I don't wanna risk running into him here."

"Girl, don't let him run you off," Valarie responds. "Fuck him and Becky!"

"Yeah, girl. I don't think you should go," Shalona responds in support of her friend.

"Thanks, y'all, but I just want to be alone right now," Iyesha says before turning her attention to Ken. "Hey, walk me out?"

Ken nods his head as Iyesha hugs both of her friends before she and Ken make their way outside of the DYA. Once there, Iyesha hands Angela to Ken with the logs and other information they have to keep track of.

"I fed her before coming here, so she should be good for a while," she explains to Ken. "Make sure you budget for more diapers on the next section. I almost ran out."

Ken notices she's talking just to keep her mind off of what happened with Chad.

"Hey. Look, I got this," he says. "I know you don't wanna talk about this right now. It's okay. I'll take care of everything."

Iyesha smiles slightly, appreciating Ken's support through everything.

"Thank you," she says. "I swear my parents warned me about these white folks. I thought Chad was different. I thought he actually loved me. I guess the joke's on me. I'm done with white folks, for real."

"Come on now," Ken responds. "You can't judge an entire race of people over one jerk."

"It's not just him, Ken. Every white person, male or female, has dogged me one way or another. They can't be trusted. I thought Chad was different, and he dogged me too. They're just evil," she responds to Ken, who shakes his head with disagreement.

"I don't believe that," Ken quips. "My best friend is white, and he's never done anything to me."

"I forget you're an Oreo cookie," Iyesha says with a hint of attitude. "You'll defend those folks till the end."

"No, just only the ones who are good to me," Ken fires back. "Look, I know I didn't grow up in what you call a black environment. I wasn't raised to break people down by color. I break them down by who's an asshole and who isn't. Color doesn't matter to me. I refuse to believe that someone is a certain type of way just because of their skin color. That's just dumb to me!"

A slight smirk enters Iyesha's face once more.

"Asshole? Really?" She says. "Don't think I've ever heard you curse before. Still a little proper and all, but I like seeing you this way."

Ken chuckles, not realizing that he did just use profanity.

"I guess when I feel strongly about something, I let it out," Ken replies.

"Doesn't mean you're right though," Iyesha points out.

"Look, I know you have white friends and all, but trust me, they will always use you and treat you as if you're inferior. You'll see that you can only trust your own kind out here. I trusted one, and he stabbed me in the back because of a fuckin' flour child. I'm never trusting them again."

Ken nods his head. He knows Iyesha is irrational now because of how emotional she is.

"Look, I know you're upset and all, but don't talk down to our daughter," Ken jokes. "Just 'cause you mad at him, don't take it out on her."

Iyesha chuckles, as Ken's words lighten the mood slightly. She walks over and hugs Ken.

"Thank you, Ken. I really appreciate it. You're such a good friend," she says before finally walking off down the street.

Ken smiles as one of the most popular girls in school hugged him and called him her friend. He had never been in the upper echelon of the school popularity crowd. Although he didn't agree with her thoughts, he still felt bad for her.

A few weeks later, in Ms. Parker's class, the bell suddenly rings, causing all the students to rush out of their final class for the day. Iyesha and Ken are walking together as she has a big smile on her face.

"First phase, A-plus," she says with a hint of cockiness. "It's all me, for real."

"Excuse me, but it takes two to raise a daughter," Ken reminds her. "I'm just saying, I did some stuff too."

"You're right, you're right. I give you props for raising your daughter. A lot of young brothas like yourself have a problem with that, so you on it," Iyesha says with a smile as they make it to her locker. "We still got a long way to go, so don't get lazy on me. Anyway, what you got going on?"

"Nothing much. Bout to head home. Might stop by the DYA, and hang out first. Not sure," Ken answers.

"You wanna go to the game tonight off base?" Iyesha asks. "We're all gonna show some support for our guys. Team is undefeated so far."

"You're going to bring our daughter to a basketball game without discussing it with me?" Ken jokes. "The audacity!"

"No crazy," Iyesha says while giggling. "My mom is gonna watch her tonight. Figured since we did so well on the first phase, we can go out and celebrate with the crew. Come on, go to the office and tell your mom you're gonna ride with me to the game. We'll get you back home, I promise you."

Ken looks on with suspicion.

"Did you even ask your mom about this?" he asks.

"Well, yes… and no," Iyesha says. "She was gonna give Shalona and Valarie a ride there, but they found a ride. I never told her that they weren't coming. So she's still under the impression that she's giving someone a ride. So why not you?"

Ken chuckles as he nods his head.

"Fine, but you're calling your mom first and making sure," Ken says with a smirk. "I mean giving two females a ride is one thing, giving a guy a ride… mom may not like that at all."

Iyesha starts laughing before leading Ken off to the office.

Later that night, Iyesha and Ken walk into the Junction City Middle School gym with the basketball game already in progress. The atmosphere is exciting as the crowd watching the game cheer after every big play. Iyesha looks around and notices her crew sitting at the far end of the bleachers. She points them out to Ken as they make their way through the crowd trying to reach their friends.

Iyesha and Ken are laughing and joking with each other. Ken is stunned as he and Hilary run into each other in the crowd. Both are speechless as Hilary is with her friend Veronica.

"Hilary? Hey," a stunned Ken says.

"Hey, Ken. How have you been?" she asks, still shocked to see him.

"Good, good. What are you doing here?" he asks.

"Here supporting my school," she responds. "I guess you're here doing the same."

Ken nods his head as Iyesha looks on silently. She can tell the two have a history with each other. There is an awkward silence when Ken remembers he's there with Iyesha.

"Oh, shit, I'm sorry. Iyesha, this is Hilary. Hilary, this is Iyesha," he says, introducing the two.

"Nice to meet you," Hilary responds, checking out Ken's new friend.

"Yeah, you too," Iyesha responds before turning her attention back to Ken. "Hey, I'm gonna head up to the crew. I'll save you a seat."

Ken nods as Iyesha walks off and heads towards Valarie, Shalona, and the others. Veronica smiles at Ken before scurrying off herself, leaving Hilary and Ken alone. Hilary has a smirk on her face as she looks at her old boyfriend.

"Well, you're looking good I see," she says. "Strutting in here with your new girlfriend. I'm impressed."

"Oh, she's not my girlfriend, she's my wife," Ken blurted out before realizing what he says. "I mean, she's my wife in this class we're in and... You know what, never mind."

"Same old Ken," Hilary replied with a sinister grin. "Well, I guess I should be glad you even acknowledged me. Last time we were together, you just went all quiet, avoiding me."

"Yeah, about that. I'm sorry," an apologetic Ken responds. "I wasn't in my right mind then, and I was wrong with it all."

Hilary is silent as she slowly nods her head.

"You really broke my heart, you realize that?" She replies. "I mean, I thought I did something wrong. I tried to figure out what happened between us, and I just couldn't put my finger on anything. Why did you do that?"

Ken sighs as he thinks for a moment.

"I guess… I don't know. There was something about what your friend says that night we all hung together," Ken admits.

"What did she say?"

Before Ken can continue, a student walks up to Hilary and hugs her from behind.

"Hey, baby," he says causing Hilary to smile as she turns and faces him.

"Hey! Me and Ronnie was just looking for you," she replies as Ken looks on with suspicion.

The student was black, confirming in Ken's mind that

Hilary and Veronica carried the same traits of liking black guys. Ken chuckles to himself as he shakes his head in disbelief.

"Hey, it was nice to see you again," Ken says. "I'll leave you two alone and head to my seat."

"No, wait a second," Hilary says. "Ken, this is Reggie. Reggie, this is my on-base friend Ken."

Reggie gives Ken a head nod before turning his attention back towards Hilary.

"You ready to go, or you staying the whole game?" Reggie asks her.

"I'm gonna jet in a few," Hilary responds. "Let me get a few ticks with my friend here. Ronnie and the others are at the end over there."

Hilary points out where her friends were to Reggie, who nods his head.

"Okay, I'll see you over there," Reggie says.

He takes a look at Ken once more before leaving the two alone once again. Ken shakes his head as if he's disappointed.

"So that's the new boyfriend I see," Ken replies.

"Yeah. We've been together for about a month," Hilary reveals. "He reminds me a lot of you, actually."

"Yeah, I bet," Ken quips back.

"Seriously, he does. He's funny, he's always nervous, quiet, and-"

"He's black," Ken responds, cutting his old love off. "That's the thing we share the most, isn't it?"

"Well, yeah, he's black," a confused Hilary replies. "Is that a problem?"

"I guess not," Ken responds. "Was he able to hook Ronnie up with a black guy?"

Hilary looks at Ken, strangely trying to understand where this line of questioning is coming from.

"What's your deal?"

"My deal is that you and your friend seem to have a taste for black guys," Ken fires back. "All that he's funny, and quiet bullshit is a joke. You liked the dude because he was black, just like the only reason you liked me was because I'm black!"

"That's not true!" Hilary says, resenting what Ken was insinuating. "I didn't like you just 'cause you're black!

Where are you getting this stuff from?"

"From Ronnie, remember?" Ken points out. "She didn't like my friend Gilbert and asked me did I have another friend to hook her up with. She specifically asked was he black. I didn't know if you were the same way at first, but I see you found another sucker to entertain you. Just proved my point."

Hilary is speechless by Ken's allegations.

"So I can't like black guys, is that it?" Hilary responds. "'Cause if you're saying that, it's sounding like you're the one with the issue here. Yes, I like black guys! There shouldn't be anything wrong with that."

"There is when that's all you seek out!" Ken exclaims. "Something tells me any black guy will do. Doesn't matter how he looks or if he has a personality! You and your friend seek black guys out like it's a game. It didn't occur to me how easily you got with me in the beginning."

A frustrated Hilary has heard enough.

"You know what? Fuck you!" Hilary says. "Go hang out with your nappy head girl. Probably pregnant like the rest of them!"

"Get out of here with all that!" Ken exclaims. "Just get out! At least I know where I stand with her! She doesn't play all these games like you and your ugly ass friend!"

Ken storms off, leaving Hilary frustrated as she watches him take a seat with his friends from a distance. Iyesha notices Ken is irritated after his discussion with Hilary as he takes a seat next to her, silently still fuming.

"You alright?" She asks, checking on her friend.

"Yeah, I'm fine," Ken replies.

"You don't seem fine. What was all that about?"

"It's... it's a long story," Ken says while sighing. "I don't want to get into it right now."

"Cool, we'll talk about it later," Iyesha says. "Right now, though. Let's have some fun! Later for the stress!"

Ken looks towards Iyesha, who is making a funny face at him trying to change his mood. It works as Ken chuckles as he begins watching the game with the others and cheering their team on.

After the game, Ken and Iyesha are standing outside the gym waiting for her mother's arrival. Ken has just explained the Hilary situation to Iyesha, who nods her head with understanding.

"I see why you were upset," she says with a slight smirk on her face. "I told you how they are, but you don't wanna listen."

"This happened before you even knew who I was," Ken says, causing Iyesha to giggle.

"I always knew who you were," she replies. "I mean, you just ran with another crowd than I did, but I know all the brothas in the school. I heard about you and Sharon a while back, how she played you for Tim. I mean, that alone should have told you to stay away from them."

Ken is surprised Iyesha knew so much about him.

"You know about Sharon? How?" Ken asks.

"Shit, everyone knew," Iyesha says while giggling. "It was all around the school. I felt sorry for you, for real."

Ken lowers his head with embarrassment, feeling like the biggest fool in the school. After a few moments, he turns to Iyesha with a hint of curiosity.

"Mind if I ask you a personal question?" He asks.

"Sure."

"With all this pro-black thing you're speaking about, how in the world did you end up with Chad?" he asks. "I mean, I've always wanted to ask you that, but I knew you were still kind of dealing with the breakup. If you don't want to answer, that's-"

"No, I'll answer," Iyesha says, figuring she might as well come clean. "I had just broken up with Ernesto. You know him from the football team, right? Played on defense?"

"Yeah, I know Ernesto. He was in my history class last year," Ken answers.

"Well, anyway, we had broken up, and I was so mad at him. I was at the DYA a few days later hangin' out with Shalona, watching her doing her cheerleading thing when Chad came over and sat by me," Iyesha explains. "Now, you know how I am. I really wasn't trying to hear anything he was saying to me, but he kept going on and on. Eventually, I opened my ears a bit and started listening. He had me laughing, and for the first time since me and Ernesto had broken up, I actually forgot about it."

Ken nods his head with understanding as Iyesha

continues.

"Anyway, after that, he kept coming around me at school, making me laugh, and buying my lunch and stuff. He treated me so good that I was starting to second-guess my view on white folks. I was like, 'maybe my parents were wrong'," Iyesha explains. "He was just so different from Ernesto in every way. I never met a guy who was into me that much. After about a month, he finally popped the question about us going together. I figured, why not. Never met a guy that sweet. Then Rebecca comes along, and you know the rest from there."

Ken nods his head, finally getting an answer to his question he had pondered since meeting Iyesha.

"So, because he cheated on you with Becky, you're gonna just erase all white guys from your future?" Ken asks.

"Yep."

"Well, Ernesto is black last I checked," Ken points out with a smirk. "And y'all broke up. Don't see you swearing off black guys."

"Let me ask you, are you running to get another white

girlfriend after what happened with Hilary?" Iyesha fires back. "I mean, everyone knows Corrina in Ms. Parker's class likes you, and you like her. I don't see you jumpin' to her."

"That's different," Ken points out. "And don't try and change the subject. Why haven't you sworn off black men?"

Before Iyesha can come up with an answer, she notices her mother's car about to pull up.

"My mom is pulling up," she says, pointing her out to Ken.

Ken chuckles as he and Iyesha walk up to the side of the curb, waiting for her mother to make it through the line of cars.

"So, a few of us are gonna hang out at the basketball court tomorrow. Nothing fancy, just chillin', you know. The two brothers from Compton are gonna be there too, and you know how they're always fighting. It's gonna be fun," Iyesha says. "You wanna come through and hang?"

"Damn, I'm staying over by my friend Gilbert's house tonight," Ken responds. "I'll be over there till Sunday."

"Cool," Iyesha says while nodding her head. "Well, have fun with that."

Ken can tell she was a little disappointed with his response. Her mother pulls up moments later as both he and Iyesha get into the car before she pulls out of the school property.

The next day, Ken is sitting in Gilbert's room with him, and his younger brother, Charles. Ken and Charles are sitting on the bedroom floor playing videogames as Gilbert is lying on the bed looking over Ken's football card collection.

"Come on, Ken. You have to trade this Elway rookie card to me," Gilbert says, admiring the card.

"No way. Do you know how much that card is worth?" Ken replies. "You can't offer me enough for it."

Gilbert sighs as he puts down the binder and watches Ken and Charles playing Tecmo Bowl.

"You never did tell me how it went with Iyesha at the game last night," Gilbert says.

"What's there to tell? We hung out, watched the game.

Nothing much really," Ken responds.

"So when are you gonna ask her out?" Gilbert questions, confusing Ken.

"Ask her out? For what?" Ken inquires. "I'm not her type, trust me."

"Are you out of your mind? You're friends with Iyesha Williams, one of the top five most popular girls in school. You received a blessing to work on this project with her, and she invites you to games and places. Do you realize what you have here?"

"Nothing, Gil. I have nothing. I'm not on her status," Ken points out.

"Maybe not, but if you and her start going together, that would change," Gilbert retorts. "The fact y'all were together would push you to a level that even I haven't reached. She likes you, trust me. I mean, why deal with you outside of school if she didn't have to unless she likes you?"

Ken shrugs Gilbert off, acting as if he's focused on the game he's playing. In the back of his mind, he considers what his friend is saying. Iyesha had invited him to the game the prior day, and a gathering taking place at the court today. Could she actually have an interest in him? Ken couldn't see himself making the first move, however. If she were to reject him, it would devastate him.

Before Ken can respond to anything, he and the others all hear Charles and Gilbert's mother and father arguing about something. Gilbert shakes his head as he and Ken try to ignore it.

"Fucking Nigger!" Gilbert's mother yells, stunning all three of them.

Gilbert and Charles look at each other as Ken remains silent, not knowing how to react to the racial slur yelled out by his friend's mother. Gilbert tries to distract the situation by grabbing the game controller from his bother.

"You skipped my turn," he says, hoping to draw attention away from what happened.

As he and his brother start to wrestle with each other, Ken shakes his head, still not knowing how to react from what he just heard. After a few moments, he rises from the floor and begins packing his items into his book sack. Gilbert notices him packing up and stops wrestling with his brother.

"Hey, where you going?" Gilbert asks. "I thought you were staying 'til Sunday."

"I was… I just… I just thought about something I need to do at home that I totally forgot about," Ken nervously says as Gilbert rises.

"Are you sure?" he asks his friend.

"Yeah, I'll call you later," Ken says as he quickly puts on his shoes. "See you."

Ken quickly walks out of his friend's room and out of the home, still stunned at what he had heard. After he crossed the street, he takes one last look at Gilbert's home before making his way down the sidewalk.

Ken is walking down the street, still replaying what he had heard in head over and over again when he looks towards the basketball court. He notices Iyesha and others hanging out, playing music while watching others playing basketball. Ken heads over towards the court, looking to check out the gathering. Iyesha's eyes light up when she saw him making his way over. She jumps up from the bench she is sitting on and runs over to him.

"Hey! What are you doing here? I thought you were gonna be at your friend's house for the weekend," she says.

"Yeah, I decided to leave a little early to come check y'all out," Ken responds, hiding the real reason for leaving. "Have the Compton brothers got into a fight yet?"

Right on cue, the two Compton brothers, who were playing basketball on the court, get into an argument over a foul and begin pushing each other.

"Looks like you came at the right time," Iyesha says with a chuckle as the two brothers start throwing punches at each other. "Come sit by us."

Ken quickly follows Iyesha over to the bench as they have a front-row seat to the altercation.

A couple of hours later, one of the crew reloads some batteries into the boom box as the music starts to play once again. Ken and Iyesha are laughing and joking with each other when Shalona walks over with a smirk on her face.

"Hey, girl," she says with a slick grin to Iyesha.

Iyesha notices the look in her friend's eye and starts

shaking her head.

"No! Shalona, you bet not do what I think you're about to do! I'm not playing with you!" she responds.

Shalona sticks out her tongue, runs over to the boom box, and loads a cassette tape into it. Ken looks on as Iyesha lowers her head with embarrassment.

"What's going on?" He asks his friend.

Before she can answer him, the boom box begins playing Another Bad Creation's *Iesha* song. The group all turn their attention to Iyesha, who shakes her head at her friends.

"Y'all know I hate that damn song! My name isn't even spelled like they spell it!" She yells with a smirk on her face while her friends start singing the song.

Everyone begins dancing to the song mocking Iyesha, who can do nothing but laugh. Ken is bobbing his head when Valarie and Shalona pull him up from the bench forcing him to join their dancing assault. Ken looks around awkwardly with a smile on his face when Iyesha turns her attention to him.

"Really, Ken? You gonna clown me too?" She says,

looking disappointed in her friend.

Ken thinks for a moment before he quickly runs over, pulls Iyesha up, and begins singing to her much to her surprise. Everyone is dancing and singing, having fun when Iyesha finally starts singing as well, relishing the attention. Both Iyesha and Ken share a look with each other before singing. The couple continues to enjoy themselves with the rest of the crowd.

Later that evening, Ken walks into his front door, still smiling after enjoying himself hanging out with Iyesha and the others when he runs across his mother, who was in the living room watching TV.

"Hey, I thought you were at Gilbert's house until tomorrow?" She asks, reminding Ken about why he left in the first place.

"Oh, yeah. No, I felt like coming home a little early," Ken replies. "It was boring over there."

"Oh, okay. Well, I wanted to talk to you anyway," she says as Ken takes a seat on the couch next to her. "Your father has decided to put in his retirement papers to the army. After the school year, we're going to move to New Orleans so we can be closer to your grandparents."

It was like a shot to the heart of Ken, who is just finding his place among the popular kids in school. What hurts him the most is he was just about to entertain the idea of a relationship with Iyesha, which seemed to show promise after the day's events. While the news is running through his head, Jermaia walks over with the cordless phone and hands it to Ken.

"Here. It's Gilbert," she says. "He's called like eight times already."

Ken nods as he walks upstairs to his room with the phone in hand before answering the line.

"Hey," he says, taking a seat on the corner of his bed.

"Hey. I've been trying to call you since you left. Just checking to make sure you made it in," Gilbert says.

"I stopped off at the court before I came home," Ken explains.

"Cool. Look, my mom wanted to apologize about what you heard earlier," Gilbert says. "She was talking about a coworker at her job, and she didn't mean to say what she said."

Ken sighs as he thinks for a moment.

"I didn't hear anything," Ken says, trying to lay the issue to rest. "So, I'm not sure what you're talking about."

"Oh, okay," a puzzled Gilbert says. "Well, my mom wanted to apologize just in case you did hear what she said."

"It's fine, really. Look, can I call you back? I just got in, and I need to run a take a bath," Ken says, trying to get off the phone.

"Oh, yeah, no problem. I'll talk to you later," Gilbert replies before Ken hangs up the phone.

Ken is exhausted as the news of his father leaving the army, and the racial incident he went through earlier has completely drained the life from him. The only thing that brought a smile to his face is the fun he had with Iyesha and her friends earlier. He reaches under his bed and takes out his songbook. He had several songs listed with different moments in his life, including the two entries for Sharon and Hilary. The Hilary entry makes him frown a bit, but he eventually moves past it. He writes down

Iyesha's name in the book, followed by her song, Another Bad Creation's Iesha. He made sure to spell Iyesha and Iesha correctly, knowing how his friend felt about it.

After a few moments, he closes the book and places it back under his bed before flopping down on his bed. He closes his eyes and reminisces about his dance with Iyesha. A smile grows on his face giving him the only happiness he's had in the last couple of days.

The school year is coming to a close as the final couple of weeks are upon Ken and his eighth-grade classmates. Ken is sitting in the lunchroom alone, picking at his food when he notices Gilbert walking in the cafeteria with a couple of his friends. He hadn't had much interaction with Gilbert since the incident at his mom's house. The once close friends were a shell of themselves. As Ken continues to pick through his food, Iyesha walks in the cafeteria and takes a seat next to him.

"Hey, husband," she says, causing Ken to chuckle.

"Hello, wife," he replies.

"Well, we did it! Highest grade in the class. I had my

doubts with you, but you came through when you needed. You're gonna make a fine husband one day," Iyesha says with a smirk.

Ken nods his head, but she can tell he's bothered by something.

"So, when were you gonna tell me?" Iyesha says.

"Tell you what?"

"That you're moving," she says, stunning Ken.

"How... how did you know that?" Ken inquires.

"I can tell," Iyesha says. "You've been a lot quieter lately, and you have that look in your eye. Oh, and Shalona was at that cheerleader thing that your sister is in last weekend, and your sister told her y'all were moving to New Orleans."

Ken starts to chuckle as Iyesha giggles as well.

"I don't know what I'm going to do," Ken says. "New Orleans isn't like anywhere I've ever been. I was there for fourth grade, and when I tell you those kids were animals... I can only imagine what it's like out there now."

"I thought it was just Mardi Gras and partyin' out there," Iyesha says.

"I wish. Those kids out there are wild. I'll probably end up shot before I get out of high school," Ken responded.

Iyesha can tell Ken is fearful about the change coming his way.

"Hey, you're not gonna get shot," she says, trying to comfort her friend. "You're too smart for that. Just always lay low, and stay outta the way, and you'll be fine. It's always the folks out there doing too much that get shot. You're not them, trust me."

Ken nods his head as he ponders for a few moments.

"I'm just going to treat it like a four-year prison term," Ken explains to Iyesha. "I just have to make it four years, and I'll be free. Away from all these drug dealers and welfare folks."

Iyesha giggles as Ken looks at her strangely.

"I'm about to go get shot and you're laughing?" Ken questions.

"No, it's not that. It's just… look, everything isn't as black and white like you make it seem," she responds. "Drug dealers and welfare folks? I mean, you have no idea what these people have gone through and are quick to judge. I'm from Philly, and let me tell you I have cousins who deal. Some people grow up in it, not knowing anything else. Some do it because there's not much else offered. I'm not saying there aren't folks out there who are doing that just because they like it, but it's not like what you think. You gotta get that white state of mind outta your head."

Ken chuckle as he shakes his head.

"Still talking about the whites I see," he says.

"And you know it," Iyesha says proudly before the smile on her face suddenly drops. "Speaking of Philly, I guess I should tell you that I'm going back home for the summer."

Ken is initially shocked but shakes his head as the news keeps getting worse.

"When do you leave?" he asks.

"Well, he said he's gonna pull me Friday since I would have taken all my tests. The final week we're not doing anything anyway," Iyesha answers, shocking Ken.

"Friday as in this Friday? I'm really not going to see you after Friday?" he somberly asks.

"No. I just found out yesterday," she replies. "I thought we would be able to hang out a little before you left, but with this news, we only have a few days left together."

Ken is speechless as both he and Iyesha share a glance. Realizing they only had a few days left with each other had the two friends struggling with their feelings.

"Damn," Ken responds.

"Damn is right," she says. "Promise me you'll walk me home Thursday."

"Sure, no problem. I will," Ken promises.

Iyesha sighs as she nods her head and rises from her chair.

"I'm about to hit the yard. You coming?" She asks.

"Yeah, I'll meet you out there. I'm just going to finish up here," Ken says, pointing to his food.

"Okay, don't take too long. We don't have much time left. Need to enjoy the time we have," Iyesha says before making her way out of the cafeteria.

Ken takes a deep breath as the news of Iyesha, leaving has him feeling sick to his stomach. His entire world is crumbling around him, and he didn't know how to feel.

Thursday quickly came as Iyesha and Ken are silently walking down the street to her home for the last time. There is a somber mood between the two knowing their time together was ending.

"So, what's the plan once you get to Philly?" Ken asks.

"I'm not sure. Guess I'll get with my cousins and see what's the plan," Iyesha replies. "Haven't thought about it. What about you? What's the first thing you're gonna do once you hit New Orleans?"

Ken shrugs, not knowing what to expect when he arrives back to his hometown. After a few more moments of silence, Ken decides to ask a question he's thought about for quite some time.

"Look, I have to ask you since this is basically our last day together. Could someone like you ever like someone like me, in the relationship sense?" He asks, piquing Iyesha's interest.

"I mean, at this point, I would hope so since you're my husband," she slyly responds.

"I'm serious. Like, would there have ever been a point when you would have considered that?" Ken asks again.

Iyesha thinks for a moment before responding.

"You said someone like me. What do you mean by that?' she asks.

"Someone popular. What did those 'say no to drugs' videos call it? Oh, the 'in-crowd,'" Ken answers, causing Iyesha to laugh.

"Boy, you're crazy. I'm not part of no 'in-crowd,' or popular," Iyesha responds.

"Could have fooled me," Ken quips back. "You're always with a lot of friends, and really could have any guy in the school you wanted. How is that not being popular?"

"I don't think about all that. And as far as having any guy in school, I don't think that's true," Iyesha answers before pondering her thoughts for a moment. "I'll be real with you, when we first started on this project, I thought you were kinda lame. I mean MC Hammer and Vanilla Ice? Seriously?"

Ken chuckles as Iyesha continues.

"Now that version of you, I could never have seen myself with. The new you, once I got to know you better... well, I guess if you would have asked me earlier, I would have thought about it," she replies. "Why did you wait till now to ask me that?"

"Like I said, your status," Ken admits. "You may not think about being popular, but you are. I didn't think you'd ever go with someone like me. How was that going to look with your inner circle?"

"You should stop worrying about how things look," Iyesha retorts. "I don't. If I like a guy, I like him. Nothing else matters."

"Says the girl who dated the captain of the football team, the defensive captain of the football team, and from what I hear Vince on the basketball team," Ken fires back, causing his friend to giggle.

"I see you've thought a lot about this," she replies.

"Yeah. If there was one normal dude on your list, I might have asked," Ken says before changing his tune. "Who am I kidding? My scary-ass wouldn't have done anything."

Both he and Iyesha laugh as they make it to the corner from her house.

"Well, it's too bad you waited so long," Iyesha replies.

"This could have been goodbye to my boyfriend."

Ken sighs as he knows the end is near, looking towards her house.

"Well, it may not be goodbye from your boyfriend, but it is goodbye from your husband. At least I can proudly say you were my wife," Ken jokes.

Iyesha nods her head before correcting Ken.

"I *am* your wife," she replies. "School year isn't over yet."

After a few moments of silence, Iyesha moves in and hugs Ken. Both are saddened, trying to hold on to this moment for as long as they can. After a few moments, Iyesha backs away with a few tears rolling down her face. Ken is full of emotions as well but can maintain for the moment.

"So I guess this is it," Ken says in a somber tone.

"Yeah, I guess it is."

"Well, have fun in Philly. Stay out of trouble," Ken responds.

"You too. Stay alive in New Orleans," she says with a grin.

Ken nods his head as Iyesha begins to walk off to her home.

"Hey!" Ken yells before she's too far off.

Iyesha turns around only to be met with Ken singing the Iesha song, causing Iyesha to burst into laughter. He starts to dance awkwardly, causing his friend to shake her head with embarrassment.

"Aye, please work on that," Iyesha says with a smile on her face.

Ken nods his head as Iyesha blows a kiss to him before walking off into her home. The smile Ken had on his face slowly starts to fade as he takes a deep breath before walking down the street towards his home.

As he's walking down the street, he notices Gilbert sitting at a nearby park bench, talking to a few of his friends. He decides to walk over and talk to the friend he had been neglecting for the past couple of months.

"Hey," Ken says as he walks over, surprising his friend.

"Ken. What's up?" Gilbert asks.

"You got a minute?" Ken inquiries.

Gilbert nods his head as he jumps up from the bench and walks over to a secluded area in the park.

"I know we've kind of been distant as of late," Ken says. "I'm sorry about that. Things just got a little hectic."

"Nah, you're good, dude," Gilbert replies. "I know why you did what you did, and I don't blame you, to be honest. I'm sorry about that."

Ken nods his head. Unlike Iyesha, he was raised to judge people by their actions, not by the color of their skin. Gilbert's mom said what she said, but that didn't mean that he was like her. It felt good to have his friend back.

"I don't know if you heard, but I'm moving this summer," Ken breaks to his friend.

"Yeah, I heard. New Orleans, right?"

Ken nods his head as the two friends remain silent for a few moments.

"Well, you're not gone yet," Gilbert responds with a smirk. "We still have some time to do all the dumb stuff we used to."

Ken smiles as well, realizing he needed to enjoy the

little time he had left with his friend.

"That's we do," he says, nodding his head. "You still running around with that fake girlfriend of yours?"

"Damn it, she was real!" Gilbert exclaims as he and Ken walk back to the bench where their other classmates were.

As they rejoin their friends, Ken and Gilbert continue to joke with each other enjoying themselves as they used to before everything broke down between them.

A month later, on Ken and his family's final day at their on-base home, Ken and Gilbert, Shalona, and Valarie were all sitting on his stoop laughing and joking with each other, enjoying their final moments together. Ken is enjoying himself, until his sister walks out of the front door with the word he had been dreading.

"Ken, mom said it's time to go," she says before scurrying back into the house.

Ken sighs as he and his friends all rise from his stoop.

"Guess it's that time," Ken says as Shalona is the first to approach him.

"H-e-ll-o, hello, hello," she says with a smirk mocking his little sister's cheer before hugging him.

"You're never going to let that go, are you?" Ken asks with a smile.

"Never," she says as Valarie is next in line.

"Ken, I got one question for you," she says with a smirk. "You down with O.P.P.?"

Ken chuckles and nods his head.

"Yeah, you know me," he says before hugging her.

"Yeah, your ass better have got it right!" Valarie says with a smirk. "By the way, Iyesha called me the other day. She wanted me to remind you to take it easy on the sistas in New Orleans. She said don't get all big-headed out there!"

Ken laughs as he nods his head with understanding. Valarie and Shalona walk off leaving Gilbert and Ken alone.

"Well, it's been fun," Gilbert says to his friend. "Just think of all the crap we've been through. I mean, I was actually one of privileged to witness the Sharon thirty-second relationship in person!"

"I would say I was privileged to meet your girlfriend at the other school, but unfortunately, she never existed, so I was never able to," Ken fires back with a smirk.

The two friends share a hug.

"Not gonna be the same without you," Gilbert says.

"Yeah, where I'm going, everything is going to change," Ken says as he takes a deep breath.

After a few moments, Ken heads into his home and grabs his backpack, which was sitting at the front door entrance. He looks around the empty home once more before making his way out into the back yard, and into his father's truck that was located in the back parking lot. After his father makes a final check, he starts the car and starts to pull off from the lot. He turns on the radio, which happens to play Whitney Houston's *I Will Always Love You*. The song touched Ken as it represented not just the crushes or girls in his life, but his entire time in Kansas. He started off-base initially for his fifth-grade year and ended his time on base with his eighth-grade year. He has grown a lot in that time. Looking back, he realized that time moved too fast. He regrets so many things, but there is a lot he experienced that made him who he was.

He takes out his songbook from his backpack and writes down 'I Will Always Love You.' He thinks for a few moments as he looks over Sharon's song, Hilary's Song, and finally Iyesha's song. He smirks, thinking about the good times rather than the bad ones. In the description next to the Whitney Houston song, he wrote 'Dedicated to Ft. Riley.' A slight smirk enters his face as he puts away his songbook and nestles his head into the car seat, trying to get some rest.

Chapter 4

The Jects (Shai - If I Ever Fall In Love) – 1992-93

A couple of months into Ken's ninth grade school year, Ken is sitting in his Civics class with his head down on his desk. Unlike in Kanas, ninth grade is still considered middle school in his new city, which means he was still a year away from officially going to high school. The transition from Ft. Riley to New Orleans has been a difficult one, to say the least. All students are required to wear uniforms, which was new to Ken. He thought of the students as animals, and the teachers treated them as such. In his class currently, nobody is paying attention to the teacher, Ms. Moore, outside of a few male students who are checking out her body. Ken is struggling to fit in with the students in his class. With his only friends being his cousin Denard, and his friend Toon, both who were two years behind him in the seventh grade despite being the same age as him.

As Ken raises his head, he does catch a quick glimpse of Mariah, who is sitting on the opposite side of the class from him. The one benefit Ken had going to his new school is there are more than enough black females for his choosing. His new crush happens to sit across from him as he watches Mariah laughing and joking with those around her, not paying attention to the lesson. He admired her perfectly smooth legs peeking down from her excessively short uniform dress. Her chocolate skin is well taken care of for someone her age, and she had a beautiful smile that shows her perfect teeth. When Mariah suddenly looked his way, Ken plays it off as if he was looking towards Ms. Moore. A slight smirk fills Mariah's face knowing that he's checking her out.

The bell suddenly rings as the overcrowded classroom empties rather quickly. Ken was packing his bag when he accidentally drops his pen on the ground. Before he's able to pick it up, Mariah crouches over and picks it up for him, leaving Ken speechless.

"You're welcome," she says, confusing Ken.

"Huh?"

"You was gonna say thank you, right?" Mariah replies as she folds her arms, looking at Ken with a slight attitude.

"Oh, yeah, I was. Sorry. Thanks," Ken says, stuttering at the first meaningful conversation he had with the opposite sex since coming from Kansas.

"Why you sound so white?" Mariah asks, catching Ken off-guard.

"I… I don't know, guess that's just how I talk," Ken nervously replies as he stands up from his desk.

"Where you from again? Like Columbia or Colorado?" Inquires Mariah.

"Kansas actually."

"Kansas boy, got it," Mariah says with a wink before walking out of the classroom.

Ken gets a good look at her going before making his way out of the classroom as well.

A few days later, Ken and his cousin Denard are out in the schoolyard hanging out when Toon walks over and joins them. Denard was slightly shorter than Ken, and dark-skinned sporting an S-curl hairstyle of the time. He and Toon, who was brown skin sporting a high top fade, were dressed in their uniforms just like Ken, but both were wearing shoes and jewelry that were against regulation. Denard smiles at a few females that walk by with his gold slugs shining, hoping to grab their attention. Ken looks around the schoolyard feeling out of place when he notices Mariah walking with a couple of her friends. Ken quickly taps his cousin on the shoulder to point out Mariah.

"Yo, Dee! That's the chick I was telling you about," he says as he points her out.

Both Denard and Toon look over at Mariah and her friends, who are standing next to the staircase in the yard.

"Who you talkin' about? Ol' girl in the middle there," asks Toon.

"Nah, man. Chick on the left. Brown-skinned," Ken replies.

Toon looks over again and nods his head as both he and Denard turn and face Ken.

"She's aight," Denard responds, shocking Ken.

"Dude! She's more than alright. She's cute as hell," he fires back.

"Ken, what the fuck?' Denard says, looking at his cousin as if he's insane.

"What?" A confused Ken asks.

"I then told you about all that cute talk, yo," Denard points out. "You not in Kansas no more. Chick's don't be cute, they be fine ouchere'!"

"What's the difference?" Ken questions, causing Denard to turn to Toon.

"Toon, school this fool please," Denard says. "Can't believe he's my cousin for real!"

Toon chuckles before looking back at Mariah and her friends.

"It's all good," he says. "She's aight for a project girl, I guess."

"Project girl?" a confused Ken asks.

"Yeah, she lives up in the Calliope," Toon replies, stunning Ken.

"You sure about that?"

"Hell yeah. Friend of mine rides home with her every day on the bus. Said she gets off on South Johnson. He was tryin' to bang her last year. So yeah, my dude, you lookin' at a project chick," Toon says with a smirk.

Ken looks over at Mariah with disappointment. In his

eyes, the projects were filled with nothing but lowlifes and drug dealers. Nothing good could come from them. As he continues to check out Mariah from a distance, he is in denial about her background and planned to get to the bottom of it.

The next day in Civics class, the teacher is going over the lesson, and once again, is ignored by the majority of her class. Ken is staring at Mariah, trying to figure her out. If she was someone who lived in the project, she was not at all what he thought project girls were. She wasn't loud and obnoxious like he envisioned folks from the project were. It was almost as if she was normal. Mariah looks up and notices him glaring at her. Ken snaps out of his glare and looks away full of embarrassment. She smirks at him before turning to one of her friends and gossiping once again.

Later that day during lunch, Ken is sitting on the stairwell out in the yard, eating some candy, and checking out the area when Mariah suddenly walks down the stairs.

She takes a seat next to Ken, surprising him.

"Hey," she says with a smile.

"Mariah, hi," a nervous Ken replies.

"That's too crazy," Mariah says with a giggle.

"What?"

"How you talk! I've been asking about you. They said your dad was in the military or somethin'," she says.

"Yeah, we traveled a lot," Ken points out. "So, you been asking about me?"

"Yeah, I been askin'," Mariah admits. "You Denard's cousin, ain't you?"

Ken nods his head.

"Yes, indeed," Mariah responds. "So do all black folks talk like you in Kansas?"

"I mean, there weren't many of us in my school," Ken replies. "I'm actually from down here. It may not sound like it, but it's true."

"You most definitely don't sound like you from down here," Mariah responds with a smirk. "So, you got a girl back in Kansas?"

"Girlfriend? No. Well, there was one, but yeah, we

kind of broke up since I was moving," Ken responds. "What about you? I assume you're from out this way."

"Born and raised, baby," Mariah says as she gets a little more comfortable.

"Really? I would have never known," Ken says sarcastically, causing Mariah to laugh.

"I see you got jokes," she quips back.

"Nah, I'm just trying to see what you're about. That's all," Ken replies with a smirk. "So, you live in the area? Down the block or something?"

"Why? You tryin' to come visit?"

"No, I'm just curious," Ken replies.

"I don't live out this way. I live in the third ward, up in the Calliope," Mariah says, disappointing Ken.

"The Calliope?" He asks, praying that he heard wrong.

"Yeah, uptown. Why?" She questions.

She can tell Ken's mood changed towards her.

"Is that a problem?" Mariah inquires with a smirk.

"No, it's cool. Just never really knew a... well, you know it's just strange, that's all," Ken stutters as Mariah catches on with what he's trying to say.

"You've never met a project girl before have you?" She asks.

Ken shakes his head, causing Mariah to burst into laughter.

"Oh my god!" she exclaims in mid-laugh. "Baby, that's too crazy!"

Ken nervously smiles as he looks around the area hoping nobody else heard their conversation. Mariah finally calms down as she wipes a few tears from her face.

"Baby, I needed that laugh," she says, looking back towards Ken. "So, you scared of me because I'm from the 'jects?"

"I'm not... no... I'm not scared," Ken struggles to say, trying not only to convince her but himself as well.

"Then why you be eyeballin' me in class all the time and not sayin' nothin'," Mariah points out to a nervous Ken.

He doesn't have an answer for her as he slowly stands up.

"Don't you lie on it either," Mariah snaps back as she rises from the stairs as well. "I know you be checkin' me out. Was wondering when you was gonna come holla at me."

"Holla at you?" A confused Ken asks.

"Yeah, say what's up, drop me a line, or somethin'" Mariah explains as she moves in closer to Ken, making him very uncomfortable. "What's the matter? Are you scared of girls?"

"Scared of girls? Hell no!" Ken fires back, knowing that he was, in fact, scared of girls.

"Then what's up?" Mariah says as she folds her arms, giving Ken that attitude vibe once again.

"Well, it's just... I...," Ken says, trying to come up with the perfect lie. "I... I have a girlfriend."

Mariah looks at Ken suspiciously.

"You just said you broke up with your girlfriend cause you moved," she points out.

"Well, technically, that's true. I mean, I said I didn't have a girlfriend back in Kansas, but... but I do have a girlfriend down here," Ken stutters, sounding like an absolute fool.

"What's her name?" a suspicious Mariah asks.

"Her name?"

"Yes. She does have a name, doesn't she," Mariah fires back.

"Of course, she has a name. It's… it's Shannon. Why?" Ken blurts out.

"I don't know no Shannon's here," Mariah points out.

"She doesn't go here. She goes to another school," Ken responds, deciding to go the Gilbert way of faking it.

Mariah isn't buying anything Ken is selling her but nods her head regardless. She could tell he was nervous around her and didn't want to press him any harder than she already has.

"Alright. That's what's up," she replies. "We can still be cool then. Don't wanna cause no beef between you and Shannon."

"You want to be my friend?" Ken says as if he was amazed.

"Christ, what's with you?" Mariah says, throwing her hands in the air. "Don't worry. I don't bite. I know you have a quote, girlfriend, but that doesn't mean me, and you can't hang."

Ken smiles before shaking his head with agreement.

"Alright, now that we got that settled, we gotta get you with the program," Mariah follows up to a clueless Ken.

"With the program? What do you mean?" He asks.

"You can't be hangin' with me like you all uppity and shit," Mariah replies. "You around black people now, and in case you don't know, you happen to be black."

Mariah grabs Ken by his arm and shows him his skin color as if she was introducing new information to him.

"Amazin', ain't it?" She says with a smirk.

Ken shakes his head as Mariah pulls him by his arm, leading him around the yard, pointing out differences between his old life and his new life. While Ken acts as if the stuff she is pointing out is common knowledge to him, some of the things she mentions on how things worked in New Orleans are very helpful with his transition.

A month later, Ken is walking to school with Denard and Toon as they update him on their day on Canal street when the cut class the previous day. Ken shakes his head, wondering why they didn't include him in their plans.

"Dude, I'm tellin' you, it was off the chain," Toon says.

"I bet it was," Ken says with a bit of an attitude. "Y'all could have told me about it."

Denard and Toon look at each other with a smirk.

'Man, you ain't about that life," Denard says. "This not your thing, trust me."

"Yeah, for real," Toon chimes in. "I mean, you got the books smart and all. You not down to hang like us."

"So cause I'm smart as you say, I can't hang on Canal like y'all?" Ken asks, trying to get an understanding.

"Let's be real, Ken. You just a good cat," Toon replies. "You probably ain't broke a law in your life."

"This fool don't cross the street unless there's a crosswalk," Denard jokes, causing Toon to laugh.

Ken frowns because he knew they were right about their assessment. The reason he wasn't fitting in with not just them, but also others in his class is everyone believes that he's a good kid. The only reason he wasn't bullied at the school was because of Denard and Toon speaking up for him. They were well respected among his classmates. Ken realizes if he's to earn his new school's respect, he's going to have to do something drastic. As they continue down the street, they're approaching a gas station, which gives Ken an idea.

"So y'all want to talk about not being down? How about I show you a way we can make some money?" Ken asks his cousin and his friend, who both look on with curiosity.

"What you gonna tell us? Invest in the stock market?" Toon responds with laughter.

"You see that gas station over there?" Ken says, pointing it out. "How about we go in there and swipe some candy? If you not too scared."

Denard and Toon look at each other as if they're offended by the notion of being scared.

"Man, ain't nobody scared," Toon fires back. "So what you tryin' to do? You wanna rob the store? 'Cause you gonna need something to hold the joint up," Toon asks.

"Rob the store? Are you out of your mind?" Ken says before explaining his plan. "No, what we're going to do is walk in, buy a candy bar, or whatever. While one of us distracts the clerk, the other one loads up on candy. Then we swap. We have one person who looks out on the outside to warn us if somebody is coming in. We do this right, and we're going to load up. Y'all in?"

Toon nods his head, as Denard is a little more hesitant.

"I don't know 'bout all that," Denard says. "Like too much shit can go wrong."

"Aw quit acting like a bitch," Toon says. "You wait outside first then if you so scary. If someone is coming, just walk in the shop so we'll know."

After a few moments, Denard nods his head with agreement.

"Alright, try and ask for something behind the counter if you can. I'll fill up first," Ken explains to Toon.

The group were all clear of the plan and head towards the gas station. Denard stays outside as Ken and Toon walk in the station and quickly look around the area. It's a small shop with candy located at the entrance. Ken drops to his knees, acting as though he's tying his shoes while Toon approaches the register.

"Yo, let me get one of those cold drinks," he says, pointing behind the register to the clerk.

As the clerk is distracted, a nervous Ken quickly loads his bag with as much candy as he can. He can feel the adrenaline rushing through his body as he tries to remain calm throughout the process. Toon keeps pointing towards different drinks confusing the clerk allowing Ken to go unnoticed. After a few moments, a relieved Ken sighs and nods to Toon, signifying he was full to capacity. Toon nods as he pays for the drink he was pointing to behind the register. A jittery Ken walks over to the register with a candy bar and is about to pay for it when he drops it behind the register on purpose to distract the clerk once again. A cool Toon quickly loads his bag with as much candy as he can before quickly exiting the store. Moments later, Denard enters the store and quickly locates the candy. Ken, who has a little glow of sweat on his head at this point, is about to point out the sodas behind the register again when both he and the clerk are distracted by what seems like a protest walking down the street. Ken snaps out his glance as he waves to Denard, who quickly grabs something and walks out of the store. Ken pays for his items and does his best to remain calm as he walks out of the station as well.

The trio starts walking slowly from the gas station when they pick up the pace. Eventually, all three of the friends start running as the adrenaline rush has them hyped up. They are laughing as they finally run out of steam several blocks down from the gas station. They take a seat at an unoccupied bus stop bench laughing at what had just occurred.

"Oh shit, that was too fun!" Toon says, trying to catch his breath.

"Hell yeah! We hit the motherload," Ken says as he opens up his book bag filled with candy.

"Who you tellin'? I loaded up back there," Toon says as he opens up his bag filled with candy as well.

As both Ken and Toon compare their loads, their attention turns to Denard, who has been quiet throughout this whole ordeal.

"What did you get?" Ken asks his cousin.

"I got a pack of Certs," Denard responds as both Ken and Toon look at him with confusion.

"A pact of Certs?" Ken asks. "Is that it?"

"Yeah. I mean y'all already took the good shit,"

Denard explains. "Wasn't much left for me to get."

"That's bullshit!" Toon exclaims. "I left all kinds of shit on there. Your ass was just too scary to get it!"

"I ain't scared of shit," Denard responded. "I just didn't have no time, that's all."

Ken smiles at his cousin and Toon's interaction. For the first time, he wasn't the one being talked down upon as if he didn't fit in. As the two continue to get riled up with each other, Ken interjects.

"Alright, alright, damn!" He says, calming the situation. "We got what we need, so let's just chill for a moment."

Denard and Toon calm down as the trio rise from the bench and start to head towards school once again. Toon is about to open a candy bar he's stolen when Ken stops him.

"What the fuck?" Toon replies.

"You're about to eat the merchandise," Ken explains. "I told you we can make money off of this. Anything you eat will cut into the profits."

"Profits? What you talkin' about?" Toon inquires.

"When we get to school, and especially at lunchtime,

we're going to sell everything we stole," Ken explains. "We didn't steal all this stuff just to eat it."

"Who gonna buy shit from us?" Denard asks. "I mean, Ms. Campbell got the mark on that shit. She be sellin' out of her classroom all the time."

"I know, but I also know she's overcharging folks," Ken points out. "She sells candy bars for like a buck. We undercut her selling for, let's say seventy-five cents. Her customers become our customers. It's as simple as that."

Denard nods his head with understanding as Toon isn't impressed.

"Seventy-five cents?" He mocks. "It's not even worth it at that amount. Besides, what happens when Ms. Campbell cuts her prices to seventy-five cents or less? And that's if she just doesn't take our shit altogether."

Ken sighs as he tries to explain his vision to both Denard and Toon.

"Okay, first, Ms. Campbell is not going to lower her prices," Ken points out. "My guess is she's buying her candy from one of the bulk selling stores. She can't drop her prices much lower because it wouldn't be worth it.

Guess how much we paid for our stash? Zero. It's all profit for us."

Toon and Denard nod their heads with understanding as Ken continues.

"Secondly, I've seen kids drinking alcohol at that one spot behind the gym," Ken points out. "Now, taking into account that even the dumbest student at school is well under the legal drinking age, we should be able to get away with what we're doing. Don't you agree?"

Toon finally understands the grand scheme and smiles as he nods his head.

"Look at K-Rock over here plannin' shit out," he responds.

"It's no big deal," Ken responds. "Ms. Campbell is still going to get her customers because it's not like we have a big supply like her. It'll just slow down a little for her."

"Sounds like a plan to me," Toon responds. "So how we gonna get the word out?"

"I think that should fall on Denard," Ken points out, turning his attention to his cousin. "I mean, if he's trying to get a cut of this, he needs to do all the marketing for us.

Not that his pack of Certs wasn't impressive."

Both Toon and Ken laugh as Denard shakes his head, annoyed by the two.

"For real, who steals a pack of Certs? Nobody's gonna buy that shit," Toon says.

Both Ken and Toon continue to give Denard a hard time as they walk to school. Ken is especially having a good time as for the first time since returning to New Orleans, he finally feels like he fits in.

Later that day at lunchtime, Ken is sitting at the bottom of his normal stairwell in the yard when a couple of students approach him. He looks around before opening his bag of goodies to present it to them. After looking at his selection, they offer him money for several items. He makes the transaction quickly as the students make their way off. Ken leans back on the stairs loving the attention that he's receiving. He's so into himself, he doesn't notice Mariah coming down the stairs and sitting next to him. As he turns to his right, he jumps when he notices a smiling Mariah sitting next to him.

"Christ girl, where did you come from?" he asks before calming himself down.

"Top of the stairs," she says with a smirk. "How you gonna be slangin' shit if you all scary?"

"I'm not scared, you just surprised me. That's all," Ken says as another student approaches him.

He goes through his transaction process once again as Mariah looks on impressed. After the student leaves, Mariah nods her head in approval.

"Look at you," she says with a smirk. "You over here looking like a corner boy slangin' that crack. You definitely then moved on from Kansas, I see."

Ken is a little bothered by Mariah's comparison.

"Corner boy slanging crack?" He says. "This is not the same thing at all. This isn't illegal at all."

"Yeah, but how you got that candy was," Mariah points out to a stunned Ken. "Oh, I talked to your cousin about it. Told me how y'all got the candy and everything. Said you set the whole thing up, which shocked the hell out of me."

Ken sighs, as he can't believe Denard is telling folks of the origins of their stolen merchandise.

"Look, I don't want to get into details, but it's not something I'm proud of," Ken responds. "I had no choice but to do it."

"Oh, and I'm sure those drug dealers you look down on didn't have a choice either," Mariah points out. "It's funny how it's cool when it's you, but somebody else, it's the devil."

"I mean, you're comparing me to a drug dealer," Ken replies with a chuckle. "Come on, you know it's not the same damn thing."

"If you say so," Mariah flippantly responds. "I know a lot of corner boys talkin' the same shit as you, sayin' they don't have a choice. To be real, unlike you, some of them don't. The whole family is in that shit, so they gotta do what they gotta do to survive. Not everything is as black and white as you wanna make it. People weren't lucky like you to grow up the way you did. They do what they gotta do to survive. So think on that before you look down on other folks."

Ken's smile drops from his face as he never considered the circumstances people live in can dictate what they become. Stealing wasn't in his nature, but he had to do what he had to walk the halls of his school. It was the only way for people to respect him. Mariah can tell her words have gotten through to him and smiles.

"Some good shit, wasn't it?" She says, referring to her advice.

"Yeah, I'm not going to lie, that was legit," Ken responds with a smirk.

"Legit enough to get a bag of skittles from you?" Mariah responds with a sly grin.

"Oh hell, naw," Ken fires back. "It's seventy-five cents for a bag."

"Are you serious? I thought we was cool," Mariah responds.

"Business is business," Ken responds with a smirk. "Besides, this isn't all mine to give."

"Tell you what, how bout I trade you?" Mariah says as she goes into her book sack and pulls out a pen. "Let me see your arm."

Ken reaches out his arm as Mariah writes her number on it, much to his surprise.

"My number's gotta be worth at least two bags of skittles, right?" a flirty Mariah says.

Ken looks at the number and nods his head in agreement. He goes into his backpack and pulls out two bags of skittles to give to her. She takes them and smiles before rising from the stairs.

"Guess I'll talk to you later," she says before walking off.

Ken is once again feeling himself. With his new hustle and the respect of the yard, Ken is finally feeling as if he belongs.

Later that night, Ken walks into his room after showering with the cordless phone in his hand. He closes his door, walks over to his backpack, and pulls out a sheet of paper where he had written Mariah's number down on earlier. He lies down in his bed and calls the number with a smile on his face. After he types in the final number, he's surprised to hear a disconnected number message on the line. He looks on confused as he hangs up and dials the number once again. After receiving the same disconnect message, he hangs up and ponders what may have happened.

The next day, Ken and Denard are at Toon's home cutting class playing videogames in the living room to pass the time. Toon comes back in from the kitchen with three scrambled egg plates and hands both Ken and Denard a plate before taking a seat on the couch next to his friends.

"Say, that hustle was pretty good yesterday," he says before taking a bite on his food.

"Yeah, not bad. We still got a nice bit left," Ken pointed out. I'm sure we'll sell out tomorrow."

"Yeah, but we outta the good shit," Toon pointed out. "I'm sold out of Snickers and Kit Kats. Down to my final M&Ms too. We need to hit a lick again and re-up."

Denard once again is hesitant but is surprised that Ken is going along with the idea of stealing again.

"Man, y'all crazy," Denard responds. "You gonna mess around and get caught, watch."

"No, we not," Toon fires back. "Look, if you not down, let me know. I'm sure me and K-Rock can run this ourselves. Ain't that right, K?"

Ken nods his head as he munches on his food.

"They weren't the brightest folks, were they?" He says with a mouth full of food. "I'm down with it, but only get stuff that sells, not Certs or anything like that."

Toon bursts into laughter, hearing the jab towards Denard.

"Man, fuck both of y'all. I'm out," he responds as he picks up the videogame controller and starts the game.

Ken chuckles to himself once more before showing concern himself. It's not what he wanted to do, but the lure of popularity in a school he desired was too much for him to overcome. He needed to keep things going, and this was the best way to do it.

A couple of months later, Ken is once again on the yard finishing his final transaction selling candy, having sold out his stash for the day. He and Toon continued their candy hustle throughout the last couple of months and were known as the 'Candy Men' of the school. They even started taking special requests for a price. Ken has a few words with Toon before breaking off from him and making his way over to Mariah, who is talking with a few of her friends.

"Hey, how'd you do today?" She says with a smirk.

"Sold out," he says proudly.

Mariah nods as she and Ken walk off to a secluded area to be alone. Ken goes into his pocket, pulls out some cash, and hands it to her. Mariah quickly counts it before putting the cash in her sock. Mariah was a good candy pusher herself, and quickly doubled Ken's candy sales. He paid her a cut for the assistance but didn't want anyone to know about it.

"So, you have to count your money now?" Ken inquires.

"Yes. I don't trust anyone when it comes to my money," Mariah fires back.

"You don't trust me? You're the one who gave me the wrong phone number, remember?" Ken reminds his friend, who chuckles.

"That was months ago, damn. Let it go already," Mariah fires back.

"Not 'til I get the real number," Ken says. "And if you give me a number to domino's or any other fast food joint, you're off the payroll."

Mariah smiles as she is impressed with Ken's aggressiveness.

"Tell you what; I'll give it to you at the sock hop today. You are going, right?" Mariah asks.

"Actually, I wasn't," Ken says. "I was going to step out and re-up for the week."

Mariah sighs as she and Ken walk back towards the yard.

"Look, not that I'm not happy getting paid and all, but how long you and Toon gonna do this shit?" She asks. "You've been different since you out here slangin' that shit."

"Different how?" A curious Ken asks.

"Well, you're missin' a lot of classes for one," Mariah points out. "You were in the National Honor Society when you first got here. Now your grades are dippin'. I'm not sayin' you can't do you, but this shit isn't you. I then told you that before. You're better than that."

"But I'm good at it," Ken retorts. "Why wouldn't you do something if you're good at it?"

"Because it only takes once for you to get caught up to lose everything," Mariah responds. "I used to think you was smart and shit. Now, you just like the rest of these dudes here. Don't throw away your life over this petty shit."

Ken thinks for a moment as Mariah's words ring true. Before he can respond, Toon runs over.

"Hey, K-Rock, you got a minute," he says.

"Yeah, what's up?"

Toon looks at Mariah, who gets the point.

"Yeah, whatever. I hope I see you later, Ken," she says before she walks off, leaving the two friends alone.

"Bad news, dude. Friend of mine went over to the gas station this morning, and they locked the doors," Toon says to a stunned Ken.

"Locked the doors? Really?"

"Yeah. We then hit them, folks, one too many times," Toon says. "We gotta keep it going, ya heard me? They have this spot on Elysian Fields I wanna check out. We can bounce out here now if you want."

Ken weighs his options while considering Mariah's words. He liked being popular and knew if the candy dried up, so would his popularity. Still, with the gas station locking their doors, it wasn't as guaranteed as it once had been. There's a battle inside of him raging on as he struggles to decide how to proceed.

Later that day, in the school's gym, the sock hop is in full effect as the DJ is playing music for the students who are packed on the gym floor. The New Orleans Bounce Style music fills the air keeping the students hype as everyone is enjoying themselves. Mariah is sitting on one of the bleachers bobbing her head to the music looking around. She's surprised to see Ken walk over next to her. A big smile grows on her face as he takes a seat next to her.

"Hey," she says.

"Hey," he responds.

"Didn't think I'd see you here," Mariah says.

"Almost didn't," Ken responds. "But, I listened to what

you were saying, and you're right. I don't need that anymore. So I came all the way over here to tell you that you're fired."

Mariah giggles as she nods her head with approval.

"Cool, very cool," she says.

"Yeah, I know. So how about that number now?" Ken asks.

"Yeah right," Mariah quips back. "You're broke now. Pretty much useless to me."

Ken shakes his head as Mariah bursts into laughter once more. The mood changes as the DJ plays a slow song, which clears the dance floor of everyone except couples. Mariah looks at Ken as a sinister grin enters her face.

"Come on. I think you deserve a dance," she says as she reaches out her hand.

"Oh, I don't dance," Ken replies.

"I don't give a damn," Mariah quips as she stands up. "Now get your ass up and dance with me!"

Ken chuckles nervously as he rises from the bleacher. Mariah leads him on the dance floor as the two slow dance together. Ken doesn't know where to put his hands on his friend, which amuses her. She takes his hands and lowers them to her backside, making him uncomfortable.

"Just relax," she whispers in his ear. "Just listen to the music and sway."

Ken follows her instructions as the two dance almost gracefully. After a few moments of listening to the song, Ken smiles as Mariah puts her head on his chest.

"This song. What's the name of this?" He asks.

"If I Ever Fall in Love. Shai sings it," Mariah answers.

"Never heard of them," Ken responds.

"Yeah, you wouldn't. Y'all were probably listening to MC Hammer in Kansas," Mariah jokes.

Ken laughs nervously as the two continue dancing. The whiff of Mariah's perfume intoxicates him as the two are in their own world for the moment. She's impressed on how elegant he's moving to say he wasn't a dancer. Ken has a smirk on his face enjoying every moment of his dance with his friend. As the song ends, he holds on to her as long as he can. The bounce music starts again as the dance floor fills back up quickly. Ken and Mariah take a step back from each other, both with smiles on their face before they join the rest of the dance floor, enjoying the more upbeat music that fills the area.

A few weeks before school is about to end, Ken has had a long year, to say the least. He's dressed more like his peers now. With his pants being more baggy and loose, unlike his usual exact fit. He's also changed his hairstyle from the normal flat top haircut to a more curled do, which is the style for the time. He's picked up a lot of the local slang as well, even though his dialect is still more proper than all of his peers. He's adapted, something he did all his years as a military brat. While he's still not fully one of the locals, he's adapted enough to fit in as best he can.

It's lunchtime, and the new Ken is standing in line, waiting for his turn to get his lunch when Toon skips the line and joins him.

"Yo, what's up?" Toon responds as he grabs a tray.

"Hey, what's up?"

"What's up is I'm about to get held back again," Toon answers. "They said I missed too much time or some shit. Either way, I was out this joint anyway. Just wastin' my time, ya heard me."

Ken nods his head in understanding as he tells the lunch lady he wanted the pizza today.

"Messed up," he says. "So you gotta do the seventh grade all over again? I mean, they can't let you do summer school?"

"Fuck that shit," a defiant Toon says. "I'm done with school. You heard about Duke. Right?"

"Yeah, somebody shot him in the projects," Ken responds.

"Yep. Since he's out of the picture, Moe and them was lookin' for some new blood, ya heard me. Said I can join the crew. Tank saw the way I was hustlin' candy up in here and vouched for me. I'm about to move up to the big leagues, for real."

Toon looks around the cafeteria cautiously before bringing Ken's attention to his belt strap. He raises his shirt to reveal he's concealing a gun. Ken shakes his head before turning his attention back to his lunch tray. He has seen so many things this year in school that he was dead to the whole situation he was witnessing. A year ago, a gun at school would have freaked him out. Now, it had just become the norm for him.

"The dope game is a lot different than the candy business," Ken points out. "You sure you wanna go there?"

"What else is there?" Toon responds as he pays for his lunch. "I mean, my mom's talking 'bout puttin' me out. I need money to make it out there. If Moe gonna take me in and let me work the block, who am I to argue?"

Ken nods his head with understanding as he pays for his lunch.

"Look, I could always use a little back up out there. You're smart and shit. I could use you to help run shit. There's good money in it," Toon says, trying to recruit his friend.

"Dude, you know good and well that ain't for me," Ken quips as he takes a seat at an unoccupied table. "Like I said, candy is one thing. Dope is a whole other thing. Folks not gettin' shot out there selling candy. I know you gotta do what you got to do, but be safe out there. We wasn't called the murder capital of the world for no reason last year."

Toon nods his head when he notices Mariah

approaching them.

"Looks like your boo is on the way," he says, pointing her out. "I'll holla at you then."

Toon daps Ken off before making his way over to another table. Mariah walks over and takes a seat across from Ken. Before he can say anything, she tears a piece of his pizza off, splitting it into two, keeping one-half for herself.

"Please, by all means, help yourself," Ken quips to a smiling Mariah.

"Anyway, I saw Toon over here talking. What's he up to?" She asks. "He hasn't been to class in a minute."

"Yeah, I think he's done with that," Ken says before taking a bite of his food. "He said he's gonna start working with Moe slangin' and shit. Said he's takin' Duke's place in the crew and wanted me to run with him."

"And you said what?" A curious Mariah asked.

"I'm not doing that shit," Ken responds as if he's offended that she would think he'd even consider it. "Do I look like somebody who could do that?"

"Nah, not really. I mean, you got the look down, but

you still talk too proper for anyone to take you seriously," Mariah responds with a smirk on her face.

Ken nods his head but is still bothered by his old friend's decision.

"It's crazy, but he's talkin' about his mom's puttin' him out. I mean, what does she think that's gonna do? She's not leaving him any options. He has a younger brother too. How's that gonna look in his eyes? Just messed up," Ken responds as Mariah finishes her potion of the pizza.

"It's funny," she says with a smile. "When we first met, you was all uppity acting like folks out there slangin' and shit was the devil. I told you then that you don't know what's behind the hustle. Now, look at you. You finally understand what the hustle is about and how it's not as black and white as you thought."

Ken nods his head in understanding, when Mariah grabs his milk off his tray, opens it, and begins drinking it. Ken looks on to her with disbelief.

"Really?" He says with a hint of attitude.

"Oh, you wanted this?" She responds with a smirk

before placing it back on his tray. "Anyway, you takin' anyone to the prom?"

"The prom? I'm not going to that," Ken responds before taking a sip of what little milk Mariah left for him. "Don't know why ninth grade has a prom. That's normally some shit the twelfth graders get back in Kansas. Then again, ninth grade is normally a high school grade out there too, so I guess it's all crazy down here."

"Okay, on the real, you have to let that go," Mariah fires back. "You're not in Kansas anymore, Toto. You're in New Orleans. This here, this is the new norm. Secondly, this is the prom, so you need to be there. They about to stop sellin' tickets tomorrow, so get you some money, and buy a ticket."

"But I don't even-"

"Lastly, have your mom bring you over to the mall and rent a tux," Mariah continues as she interrupts Ken. "They may not have a big selection since you waitin' to the last minute, but don't show up in no regular shirt and tie shit, or I'm gonna rib the hell outta you."

Ken chuckles as he shakes his head. Mariah can be a

bit bossy at times when she wanted to have her way. Just as he does most of the time, he caves in to her request.

"Fine," he says. "So, I assume you're goin' with someone since you're over here questioning me about it."

A smirk enters Mariah's face as she nods her head.

"Yeah, I'm going with Ken," she says before clarifying. "Not, you, but Ken in my English class. You know him, the one with the glasses."

"Yeah, I know who you're talking about," Ken responds as he looks at her with confusion. "He's in my music class. Always runnin' around like he's Malcolm X and shit. He even told us to call him Ken X now. Are you serious goin' to the prom with him?"

"Well, he asked, and I said yes," Mariah responds. "It's not like anyone else asked me out."

"So, you just go out with anyone who asks?" Ken says mockingly.

"Fuck you," Mariah says with a smile. "Well, you need to find you a date then. What about that one girl who likes you? What was her name? Natalie?"

"She got put out last week," Ken points out. "She

stabbed Ms. Tate with a pencil."

"Oh shit, I heard about that!" Mariah responds. "Shit, that was her?"

Ken nods his head as a stunned Mariah is still in disbelief. They continue to discuss their plans for the upcoming prom. Mariah suggests several prom options to Ken, who shoots them all down for one reason or another.

In a downtown New Orleans Hotel three weeks later, the ninth grade prom is underway. Students are dropped off by their parents wearing elegant gowns or tuxedos. As they enter into the hall area, you can hear the loud music banging throughout. Ken walks in wearing an all-white tux, with a red cummerbund and red tie. He's very fidgety as he doesn't like long sleeve shirts. As he walks towards the hall entrance, he's stunned to see Denard and Toon standing just outside the hall door entrance. Both are decked out in their tuxedos as well and smile when they see Ken walking over.

"Look at this fool, looking clean as a mutha," Toon says as he daps off a confused Ken.

"What are y'all doin' here?" Ken asks. "Y'all are in the seventh grade."

"Dude, money is money," Denard replies. "School will take anybody money. A ten-year-old could be up in here. We didn't think you were coming."

"I wasn't. Mariah talked me into it a few weeks back," Ken admits as he and the others enter into the hall.

The hall was very spacious with a DJ at the far end playing music. There was a small dance floor area and a refreshment area as well.

Ken, Denard, and Toon all take a seat at an unoccupied table.

"So Mariah talked you into coming?" Denard asks. "Then why y'all didn't come together?"

"She talked me into coming, but she wasn't coming with me," Ken points out. "She's coming with the other Ken. The one who acts like he's in the Nation of Islam."

"Yo, wait a minute. So you mean to tell me she coming with a dude who has the same name as you?" Toon says with a chuckle. "Aye, I gotta give shorty her props, ya heard me. She's a playa for real."

Ken shoos Toon as they look around the dance floor to see who is with who. After a few moments, Denard taps Ken on the shoulder and points out Mariah, who has entered the hall attached to the arm of her date, Ken X. She's wearing a beautiful blue and white gown with white heels and her hair pinned up. Her face is slightly touched with makeup, which is out of the ordinary for her. She smiles as she greets several people before noticing Ken and his table group.

"Look at this shit. He's coming to the prom with your ol' lady," Toon says.

"She's not my ol' lady," Ken fires back.

"She's definitely not tonight anyway," Denard responds as he and Toon start laughing.

Mariah walks up to them, still attached to Ken X's arm.

"Gentlemen. I assume you know my date, Ken," Mariah says with a proper dialect.

"What's up my brothas," Ken X says as he daps each of them off.

Ken looks at his competition and is unimpressed.

"How long y'all been here?" Mariah asks.

"Just got here not too long ago," Toon responds.

"Alright, well, we're gonna go and holla at folks. I'll see you around," Mariah says before leading Ken X away from the group.

Before she leaves, she glances at Ken, who doesn't make eye contact with her.

A couple of hours later, Ken is at the refreshment table picking through the leftover food, when he notices Mariah sitting alone, looking upset. He thinks for a moment before walking over towards her.

"Hey," he says, noticing her mood.

Mariah looks at him with an attitude.

"Oh, so now you come and speak?" she fires back.

"Well, you was with your man, so I didn't wanna mess up y'all thing," Ken replies to an irritated Mariah.

"He's not my man," she quips.

"You're at a dance with him, right?" Ken points out. "I mean y'all came together. What else should I call him?"

"Don't call him shit, 'cause I cussed his ass out!" Mariah says, almost on the brink of tears. "He kept tryin' talk me into hookin' up with him. It's the only reason his dumb ass asked me out, thinkin' we were gonna fuck."

Ken sighs as he takes a seat next to his friend, trying to comfort her.

"I'm sorry," he says.

"Don't apologize. You didn't do it," Mariah responds. "I should have known not to mess with his dirty dick ass! Fake ass Malcolm X bitch!"

Ken chuckles, as he's never seen his friend so riled up.

"Damn, tell me how you really feel," he jokes as Mariah loosens up a bit.

"I'm sorry. It's just I'm not gonna be pressured to have sex," Mariah replies. "I ain't the one to play that shit with."

"Well, tell you what. Why don't we just sit here and enjoy the rest of the night," Ken says as he gets comfortable in his chair. "I promise you, I won't mention sex not one time. Scouts honor."

Mariah looks at Ken with a smirk as he holds his hand up with his fingers crossed.

"Um, I know I ain't the smartest girl in the world, but I don't think your fingers are supposed to be crossed," she points out.

"Damn, I was hopin' you didn't catch that," Ken responds with a smile.

"See, don't have me ditch your ass too," she playfully responds.

The two are laughing when *If I Ever Fall in Love* by Shai suddenly fills the hall. Several couples go to the floor and begin dancing with each other. Mariah turns to Ken and reaches out her hand.

"What?" Ken asks.

"This is our song," Mariah points out. "I came to the dance to actually dance. So, will you do me the honor?"

"*Do me the honor?*" Ken responds with a chuckle. "That's not talkin' black like you used to tell me."

"I was tryin' to be polite," Mariah responds. "You're right though. So let me rephrase. Get your ass up out that chair and dance with me!"

"Now that's the Mariah I know," Ken says as he rises from his chair and leads her to the dance floor.

For this dance, Ken is more comfortable as he places his hands on her backside. Mariah puts her head on his

184

chest as the two enjoy the moment. As he's dancing, Ken notices both Denard and Toon in the background giving him thumbs up. He chuckles to himself as he and Mariah continue to gracefully dance.

After the song ends, Mariah takes a look at her friend and can tell he's distant.

"Hey, you still there?" She asks.

"Huh?"

"You was trippin' for a moment there. Everything good?"

Ken nods his head as a smile grows on his face.

"Yeah, I'm good," he responds.

As they make their way off the dance floor, an idea hits Mariah.

"Say, let's go take pictures before the guy leaves," she says while leading Ken over to the picture line.

"Are you serious?" Ken asks.

"Yes! The dance is almost over. How do I look?" Mariah says as she straightens her dress out.

"You look nice," Ken replies to a disappointed Mariah.

"I look nice? Just nice?" She responds with an attitude.

"You look good. Cute. Fine. I don't know, you look whatever you need to hear to get that look off your face," Ken replies, causing Mariah to giggle.

The two wait patiently in line to take their picture together. Once it's their turn, Mariah makes sure she and Ken are close as the two pose with each other. The tux he's wearing and the dress she's wearing doesn't match, but it didn't matter. All that matters is that they were together. They both smile as the picture is snapped, capturing the moment for years to come.

Later that night, Ken walks in his room and immediately takes off his tux jacket and a button-down shirt. Once he's comfortable he reaches under his bed where he normally keeps his most treasured items and pulls out his songbook. He opens it up and writes Mariah's name in there, and adds their song into it. It's the second time they've danced to it, so it was officially their song and deserved recognition in the great book. After a few moments, he closes the book and begins to take the rest of his tux off to turn in for the night.

Chapter 5

Slave to Reality (Ace of Base - The Sign) - 1994

Ken's ninth-grade year brought him all sorts of struggles. In his tenth grade year, however, he felt things would be different. He's finally in high school and has had a year under his belt to get adjusted to his surroundings. While he still feels like an outsider at times, he can blend in enough to go unnoticed which is what he wanted. He didn't have Denard or Toon to vouch for him now, so he has to carry himself on his own. He's adjusted pretty well and the school year is going better than he had hoped. It's late fall, and Ken finds himself playing chess with Walter, one of his classmates, in his English teacher's classroom during lunch. It was the only place that he and others like him could get away from the others and enjoy discussions and games such as chess that would get them ridiculed by their classmates. Walter makes the final move on the board putting Ken in checkmate, much to his displeasure.

"Son of a bitch," Ken responds as he checks the board to make sure there was no other way out of the trap his friend had set.

"Sorry, Ken. I keep telling you that you bring your queen out too early," Walter says with a smile. "Keep trying, I'm sure you'll beat me one of these days. Who's next?"

Ken shakes his head as he rises from his seat to let another player step in. Walter is the only person in the group Ken couldn't beat in chess. He takes a seat to watch the next player up, hoping to get a little insight on how to beat the eleventh-grader.

Later that day, in Ken's final class, he and his peers are sitting at their desks working on different projects in their drafting software when a new student walks through the door. The student catches everyone off guard as she walks to the front of the class with Mr. Scalise, the drafting class teacher. After a few words, he gets everyone's attention.

"Everyone, I'd like to introduce a new student to the class, Victoria," he says to the stunned students. "Seems like she got a little lost today, and couldn't find us. She's here now, so please, welcome her. Victoria, you can take any available computer."

The class is dead silent as they watch her take a seat in the back corner. The reason the class is stunned is that Victoria is white. There are only a handful of white students in the school, and they weren't treated kindly by the other classmates. Ken is the only student not too worried about it. Reggie, who is sitting next to Ken, scoots over and leans in.

"Can you believe this shit?" He says to Ken. "Her parents must be trippin' or something."

"Why you say that?" Ken asks as he turns and looks at Victoria.

"'Cause ain't no way they in their right minds sending their daughter to this school. No way," he explains.

"I mean, if she lives in the district, they gotta take her, right?" Ken asks.

"Yeah, but you know them white folks be having money," Reggie responds. "They could have afforded to send her ass somewhere, I'm sure."

"Dude, please. Believe it or not, not all white folks are rich," Ken responds as he turns back to his computer.

"Money isn't about race, trust me."

"Man, whatever," Reggie says before turning back towards his computer.

Ken peeks at Victoria again and notices she looks a little out of place amongst the rest of the students.

As class ends, all the students rush out of the classroom, happy that the day is over. Ken notices Victoria is still packing her things and decides to introduce himself.

"Hey," he says as he approaches. "How was the first day?"

Victoria smiles as she looks up at Ken.

"Crazy. This is going to take some getting used to," she replies with a proper dialect.

"I bet it is," Ken says, using his Kansas dialect. "I'm Ken, and trust me when I tell you that I've been there before. Just last year."

"Hey, Ken. Look, I know that you're trying to be friendly, and I appreciate it, but you have no idea how it feels to be me right now," she responds as she grabs her book sack.

"Let me guess, you feel alone," Ken replies, piquing Victoria's interest. "You feel why me. Why was I dropped into this hell hole? I bet you're even thinking that all you have to do is survive the next two to three years, and you can leave all this behind. Am I close?"

Victoria is stunned and speechless with Ken's words. As he checks her out, she reminds him of Sharon slightly from back in Kansas, just a little more mature. Her uniform is exposing her shape, which was sexy, in his opinion. She has dark brown hair that is slicked a little, hanging down to her shoulders. She has a little lip balm on, but outside of that, she is makeup-free. Ken knows how she felt and is hoping to make her transition a little better than his was.

"You... you're not too far off," she says with a smile. "May I ask how you know all that?"

Ken chuckles as Victoria rises from her desk.

"Let's just say I've been trying for the last year and a half to fit in, and I'm still not there," he responds as the two make their way out of the classroom.

Moments later, they are walking outside of the school

gates, still getting to know each other. Ken learns that Victoria is from Utah and has just moved into the area. Her father's job relocated him, and he enrolled her in the district school that was closest to their home. Before fully enrolling, however, she followed Ken's path as she took several tests to get into more prestigious schools, but because the school year was already underway, she was put on the waiting list. Ken was put on the waiting list to one of the schools as well. He was offered a spot a week after school had already started. Ken decided to stay where he is because it made his home commute and easy one, only needing to catch one bus to get back home. Mariah and a few others he knew from middle school also attended, so he was comfortable with the atmosphere. He can tell Victoria is nervous as she looks around at all the students in the area. Ken chuckles as they make it to the bus stop in front of the school.

"Let me guess, there weren't too many black folks in your school back in Utah?" Ken asks.

"No, not really," Victoria answers. "And don't get me wrong, I'm not saying that there's anything wrong with here, it's just… I don't know, different."

"Like I said, I totally understand," Ken says. "If it was a culture shock with me, I'm sure it has you terrified. There's nothing wrong with that at all."

Victoria nods her head, but Ken can tell she's still a little nervous.

"Tell you what, why don't I help you get acclimated to the school?" Ken offers. "I mean, I'm nowhere near the most popular guy in school, but maybe I can help you get into your flow. Who knows, maybe you'll come to like it."

Victoria giggles as she slowly nods her head, accepting Ken's proposal.

"I'd like that," she replies.

"Cool, you have first lunch or second lunch?" He asks.

"Second."

"Perfect, so do I. Let's say we meet in the cafeteria at lunch tomorrow," Ken responds. "I'll help you get through this with as little pain as possible. Well, hopefully, I will."

Victoria nods her head with a smile on her face when Mariah notices him and Victoria talking and makes her way over.

"Yo, Ken," she shouts, drawing attention to them as she walks over.

"Hey, what's goin' on?" Ken inquires to Mariah.

"Nothin' really. Was just checkin' to see what's good," she answers as she checks out Victoria.

"I'm cool," he says before introducing Victoria to her. "Hey, this is Victoria. She's new to the school. Victoria, this is my friend, Mariah."

Victoria smiles and reaches out to shake hands. Mariah is cautious as she shakes Victoria's hand.

"Hey," Mariah responds with no enthusiasm.

"Hey. It's nice to meet you," Victoria responds when she notices her bus is coming down the street. "That's me there. Thanks, Ken, for everything. I'll see you tomorrow at lunch."

Ken nods his head as Valeria waves to Mariah before running off. Mariah is confused as she turns to Ken.

"Okay, what's with the white girl?" She asks.

"What you mean, what's with her? She's new to the school. Met her in my drafting class," Ken responds as he walks over and takes a seat at the bus bench once everyone has cleared out.

Mariah takes a seat next to him, still trying to get to the bottom of things with her friend.

"So you said. What's with all that 'I'll see you tomorrow at lunch' bullshit?" she fires back with an attitude. "I mean, I can't get a lunch with you, and in less than a day, the white girl got you ready to slave for her. Speaking of which, where were you at lunch today? In your little chess club?"

Ken grabs his head in frustration as he knew Mariah would have issues with him and Victoria.

"Okay, first off, I'm not in a damn chess club," Ken points out. "I just meet a few folks and play chess every now and then."

"Can everybody in the class play chess?" Mariah quips.

"Well, yeah, but it's not like-"

"Then, it's a chess club!" She exclaims.

Ken shakes his head and sighs before continuing.

"Secondly, I told her I'd meet with her at lunch to help her ease in," he says. "You don't know how it is trying to fit in where you're not wanted. Y'all New Orleans folks make shit difficult, I swear."

"Ken, I know you think you're doin' her good and all, but you need to watch that shit," Mariah warns. "You get too friendly with the white folks, people are gonna notice. You don't wanna be known as the Oreo of the bunch, trust me."

"And why is that?" Ken fires back. "I mean, really, the only thing I'm doing is talkin' with the girl. It's not like we're together or shit. And for argument's sake, say that we were. What's the big deal?"

"The big deal is she's white, Ken! We don't fuck with their kind. Look at history, how they treated us. Well, I should say treat us cause it's still goin' on," Mariah responds. "These white folks treat us like shit through all walks of life, but expect us to be all welcoming and shit when they need us? Get the fuck outta here with all that."

"Not all white folks are racist," Ken responds. "Just like not all black folks are criminals. I don't see what the big deal is. We're all people when you come down to it. This is the dream Martin Luther King Jr. had, remember?

Whites and blacks living together, being equal."

"The problem is we're not equal to them," Mariah points out as she rises from the bench. "And we're not in Kansas. This is Malcolm X down here. That dream don't exist."

"Even Malcolm changes his thought process around the end," Ken quips.

Mariah sighs and shakes her head as she walks off, leaving Ken sitting alone.

He didn't understand the big deal of helping someone else out, but he's heard that mentality before back with Iyesha in middle school.

The next day, during lunchtime, Victoria is sitting alone in the cafeteria, noticing several students looking at her from a distance. She feels uneasy until Ken walks over with his tray of food and takes a seat across from her. She greets him with a smile, happy to see a friendly face.

"Hey. I was beginning to think you stood me up," she says before taking a sip of her milk.

"Nah. I have one of those teachers who likes to make a

point at times that she's in control, so she tells us the bell doesn't dismiss us, she does and makes us sit there until she feels like letting us out," Ken responds before digging into his food.

"Yeah, these teachers are a little rough out here, aren't they?" Victoria asks.

"Trust me, you have no idea," Ken replies with a smirk. "Although I get it sometimes. For example, we had a substitute last week in my Science class. This poor guy didn't know what he was getting into. He stepped out of the class for a moment, and someone locked the door on him."

Victoria is stunned as Ken takes a few bites of his food.

"You're joking, right?" She asks.

"Nope. He kept banging on the door, but nobody would let him back in. He stood there for about twenty minutes until finally deciding to get the janitor to unlock the door," Ken explains with a chuckle. "I mean, when I first got here, I thought these teachers were rough, but after dealing with the students, I can kinda understand."

"Why didn't you open the door for him?" She asks,

causing Ken to stop in mid-bite.

"Are you kidding me?" He responds with a smirk. "Trust me, you don't wanna be that kid that sides with the faculty. I'm not tryin' to get my ass beat over helping out a teacher. Besides, it was funny to see him try everything he could to get back into the classroom."

Victoria nods her head, but Ken can tell she's not satisfied with the answer he's given her.

"Look, I'm not a bad guy. Sure, I think what they did to him was wrong, and he probably got in trouble for it," Ken explains. "But I don't have the juice to do things like that. I had to work my way up from being an outsider to a mildly respectable dude. I go around being teacher's pet, and I'm right back where I started. Where you're at now."

Victoria nods her head once again as she sighs, still noticing people leering at her.

"I get it. Trust me, I do," she says. "Everyone's looking at me like I'm a freak. I'm surprised you're even bothering with me. I mean, isn't this going to hurt your rep?"

"Nah, they've been calling me white since middle school. Nothing's gonna change that regardless," Ken explains with a chuckle. "If anything, this will give them more ammunition, but I'm past all that at this point."

"Yeah, I guess," Victoria responds, feeling hopeless. "At least you can blend in. All these eyes on me… it feels spooky, you know."

Ken sighs, understanding how it must feel being in her position. When he was the outcast in middle school, he felt the same way, but like Victoria pointed out, at least he was able to blend in a little. With her being white, there was no way to hide from the uneasy feeling of people looking at her, making her feel uncomfortable. After a few moments, a thought crosses his mind.

"Say, you wouldn't happen to know how to play chess, do you?" He asks.

"A little bit," she responds, causing Ken to smile. "My dad was trying to teach me. I know the basics, but I'm no Bobby Fischer."

"The fact you know who Bobby Fischer is works," Ken replies before quickly finishing up his food. "Come on, follow me."

Ken rises from his seat and grabs his tray as a confused

Victoria did as well. She grabs her tray and quickly follows Ken.

Around fifteen minutes later, Ken watches as Victoria is in the middle of a chess game with Mr. Jenkins, his English teacher. Before anyone can hang in his classroom during lunch, they must play him to show they have at least the most basic knowledge of chess. After a few more moves, Mr. Jenkins places her in checkmate ending the game. Ken awaits his answer as Mr. Jenkins thinks for a few moments.

"She's going to need a lot of work, Ken," he says to his student. "Think you're up to the task?"

Ken and Victoria look at each other and chuckle.

"Yeah, I can get her up to speed," he responds.

"Alright. Well, Ms. Victoria, welcome to the club," Mr. Jenkins replies as he shakes her hand.

"Thank you," a happy Victoria responds.

Ken collects the chessboard and pieces from Mr. Jenkins' desk, walks over to a desk, and sets the board up once again. Victoria smiles as Walter, and the other students welcome her to their club. After a few moments, she walks over and takes a seat across from Ken.

"Thank you," a grateful Victoria says.

"Hey, I'm happy you knew how to play 'cause Mr. Jenkins don't mess around," Ken responds. "He beat all of us coming in here, so we're trying to see who will be the first to actually take him out. I came close, but everyone knows I bring my queen out too early.

Victoria nods as she makes the first move on the chessboard.

"So, you meet here every lunch?" She inquires.

"Yeah. Well, no. I don't every day. Sometimes I hang out with a few folks during lunch," Ken responds as he moves his piece.

"Like your friend from yesterday?" Victoria asks.

"Yeah. I tried to get her up in here, but she doesn't know how to play, and she doesn't wanna know how to play," Ken responds. "She's moody like that."

"I can tell," Victoria responds. "She didn't seem to like me."

"Yeah, don't sweat that," Ken responds with Mariah's

speech from the day before still in the back of his mind. "That was more about me than you. Trust me."

"Interesting," Victoria responds as she makes her move.

As they continue to play their game, Mr. Jenkins takes a look at the time.

"Alright, we have about five minutes, everyone. Make sure you pick up your messes," he says, alerting the students.

Everyone gets up and begins straitening up their area. Ken picks up the game board and pieces and places them back in the box as Victoria straightens out the seats they were in.

"So, I guess this will be my spot for the foreseeable future," she says with a smirk. "Hiding from those prying eyes."

"Yeah. The folks here are cool. Not as judgmental as some," Ken admits as he looks around the area. "Seems like we're set. So, I'll see you in seventh period?"

"Yeah, I'll see you there," she says before walking off.

Ken checks her out as she walks off and nods his head

with approval.

"Finally, all the black women in the world to choose from, and I'm back hanging with white girls," he softly says to himself.

He chuckles for a moment before grabbing his bag and making his way out of Mr. Jenkins' class as well.

Hours later, Ken is walking down the school hall when he notices Victoria walking down the hall as well. She's wearing some headphones listening to music, which surprises Ken. He quickly makes his way over to her.

"Hey, what are you doing?" He asks, surprising Victoria.

"Hey. What do you mean?" She replies.

"Them headphones. Take them off, quick," he says as he looks around the area.

A confused Victoria quickly takes off her headphones and puts her Walkman into her book bag.

"What happened? What did I do?" She asks.

"Headphones are a no-no," Ken responds as he continues to look around. "For two reasons. One, they're not allowed. If one of the teachers catch you, they'll confiscate them. Secondly, you can make yourself a mark. Someone sees you with that, they could get it in their head to want to relieve you of them. You follow me?"

Victoria is speechless as she slowly nods her head.

"I know that this seems odd," Ken says as he and Victoria continue down the school hall. "But I keep tellin' you, it's not the same as where we came from."

"I've seen a lot of students wearing them though," she points out. "I didn't know it wasn't allowed."

"I'm sure you see a lot of students playing spade, tonk, and pitty pat too," Ken reminds her. "I know you've seen dudes rollin' dice around the gym. None of that's legal, so to speak. Folks always gonna do things, but it only takes one teacher to have a bad day to enforce it. Besides, like I said, that's the least of your worries. The jackers are the ones you really should be worried about. You are an easy target, and if any of them catch you, they will steal your shit."

A terrified Victoria nods her head as the two make it to their drafting class. Ken opened her eyes. Once she gets to her desk, she immediately takes off her jewelry and places it into her book bag. She looks around the class at the other students hoping that none of them are looking her way.

As the class continues, Victoria has loosened up a bit, laughing and joking with a couple of students, including Ken who is happy to see her fitting in so well. Mr. Scalise steps out of the class for a moment as the students congregate with each other.

"So be real, Vikki," Reggie says with a smile on his face. "I heard white folks in Utah all have like multiple wives and shit out there. Is that true? Cause if it is, then a brotha needs to relocate. You know what I'm sayin'."

Victoria bursts into laughter as Ken shakes his head, embarrassed for his friend.

"Just stop it," Ken butts in. "You sound like the same dude who asked me did I ride around on horses in Kansas. You do know how stupid that shit sounds, right?"

"Hey, I don't hear her denyin' the shit," Reggie says with a smile as he looks back to Victoria. "Vikki, come on now, baby girl. Tell the truth."

Before Victoria can respond, a student walking by the

classroom peeks his head in the door and notices Mr. Scalise is gone.

"Yo, anyone got a problem?" The student says, raising his shirt to reveal he's strapped with a gun.

The class goes quiet because the student has everyone's attention.

"Anyone? Y'all got a problem?" He repeats as everyone continues to look on in silence.

The student chuckles as he lowers his shirt.

"Y'all a bunch of hoes," he says before walking off.

After he's gone, everyone turns back to their discussions except Victoria. She can't believe how everyone just brushed off what had just happened. A few moments later, Mr. Scalise returns to class and takes a seat back at his desk. Victoria is about to approach him when Ken and Reggie gently pull her back down in her seat.

"I know you not 'bout to do what I think you 'bout to do," Reggie says before turning his attention to Ken. "Yo, Ken. You need to holla at your girl, for real."

Ken nods as Victoria turns her attention to her friend.

"Holler at me? About what? You did see that guy had

a gun, right?" She inquires.

"Yeah, I saw it, but you gotta keep quiet," Ken warns.

"How can you keep quiet? He could shoot someone," a confused Victoria replies.

"True, he could, but what do you think he'd do to the person who rats him out?" Ken points out. "They not gonna put you in some witness protection program. If they catch him, and if he still has the gun on him, maybe they take him to juvie. Maybe he has one of his friends come after you once he finds out it was you that ratted on him. You gotta think about all that."

A stunned Victoria is conflicted with her thoughts about doing the right thing as opposed to ignoring what happened. Ken made some valid points she hadn't thought about. Still, the fact that nobody was bothered with what they saw still disturbs her. After pondering her options for a few moments, she slowly nods her head agreeing to keep what she saw quiet. Both Reggie and Ken look at each other, relieved that she decided to back down.

After the bell rings, Ken and the other students all rise

and prepare to leave for the day. Ken can tell Victoria is still bothered by the earlier events and tries to calm her down.

"Hey, you okay?" He asks.

"Yeah, it's just... things can't be like this, can they?" She asks.

"Sadly, it is. I'm not gonna lie to you, this is like the norm," Ken replies.

"How did you deal with it?" She asks as Ken thinks for a moment.

"I don't think I ever really dealt with it," Ken admits as the two walks out of class together. "I just accepted this is the new norm and moved on. It's not like the movies. One person can't make a difference. Well, some can, but nobody like us. Someone who's been here their whole life can."

Victoria nods her head with understanding even though she's still bothered with everything. As they make it to the front of the school, they are joined by Mariah, who shoots Victoria a look before turning her attention to Ken.

"Hey, did you hear about Jellyroll?" She asks.

"That's his name! Jellyroll! I couldn't think of it," Ken responds before turning his attention towards Victoria. "He's the dude that was flashin' the gun earlier."

Mariah nods her head as the trio walk towards the bus stop in front of the school.

"Yeah, he was flashin' it alright. In the yard during lunch, he was stuntin' talkin' mess to Fish. Even pulled the gun on Fish in front of everybody!" Mariah responds, stunning Victoria.

"Wait, he pulled the gun out on someone?" she asks Mariah.

"Yeah. I was in the middle of the shit too," Mariah answers. "Jellyroll was on one side of the yard, and Fish was on the other side. They was talkin' shit to each other when Jellyroll pulled out the strap on Fish and his crew. Fish didn't back down either. It was crazy for real. When me and a few folks realized we was in the middle of the yard between them, we backed the fuck up real quick just in case that fool started blastin'."

Victoria turns to Ken, who waves her down, knowing what she was thinking.

"And this was at lunch?" Ken asks.

"Yeah, surprised you didn't hear about it. Probably was all into your chess game to notice," Mariah pokes back with a smirk. "You know you chess club folks don't get the latest gossip."

Ken shakes his head and is about to respond when Victoria cuts him off.

"Ken, we need to tell somebody," Victoria says. "I mean, if he's pulled the gun out on someone, he could kill someone!"

"Well, I don't think that's gonna happen anytime soon," Mariah responds with a smirk. "About fifteen minutes ago, Fish and his crew caught Jellyroll slippin', and when I tell you, the whole Gentilly neighborhood jumped on that boy, baby. Wooo."

Ken shakes his head as Victoria looks on in disbelief.

"They... they jumped him?" she asks.

"Yep. I ain't never seen someone get they ass beat that bad," Mariah points out. "He kept tryin' to go down and cover-up, but them folks kept holdin' him up makin' sure he felt all that shit. A friend of his kept tryin' to help him

211

out, but they just pushed him to the side like it he wasn't nothin'. You have no idea how deep Gentilly runs up in here. My whole class ran outside and watched that ass whoopin'."

"Wait a minute. I'm trippin' here. Fish don't even go here, do he?" Ken inquires. "I remember him in middle school, but he don't go here."

"Nope, but when fools have beef, you think a school gate gonna stop them?" Mariah responds, but Victoria is still not satisfied.

"The guy, the one with the gun. What happened with him after the fight?" She asks.

"I don't know. I think they called security to break up the fight, but outside of that, I don't know," Mariah responds as Victoria looks at Ken nervously.

"What if he comes back? I mean, what are we going to do if he-"

"Hold up, wait a sec. What do you mean, we?" Mariah interrupts. "That shit don't have anything to do with us, and it definitely doesn't have anything to do with you. So, why are you trippin'?"

Victoria shakes her head in denial as Ken waves her off once more, trying to calm her down.

"Look, just chill for a minute," he tells her when he notices her bus has arrived. "Your ride's here. Just go home right now and clear your head. We'll talk on it tomorrow."

Victoria takes a deep breath before slowly nodding her head in agreement. She walks over and gets on the bus as Mariah giggles to herself.

"Baby, she's not gonna make it here if she's trippin' on shit like this," Mariah responds.

"The shit is new to her, Riah. Cut her some slack," Ken quips.

"Look at you, takin' up for your boo," Mariah jokes with a smile on her face. "So it seems you can take the boy outta Kansas, but you can't take the Kanas outta the boy."

Ken frowns as he's heard enough from his friend. He shoots her a look before walking off, leaving her standing alone, which stuns her. She's about to go after him but decides to back down and give her friend some space.

A few weeks later, Ken walks into Mr. Jenkins's classroom at lunch and notices Victoria sitting at a desk with the chessboard already set up. She has her headphones on bobbing her head, listening to music. Ken chuckles as he walks over and takes a seat across from her.

"I see you not gonna learn about them headphones," he says as she removes them.

"Hey. Mr. Jenkins said he was cool with it, and I don't think there are any jackers as you call them in here," she replies with a smile as she moves first on the chessboard.

"Who knows, I may be one of the jackers," Ken replies with a smirk before he moves.

"Please," Victoria says with a chuckle before moving once again. "Mariah said you wouldn't hurt a fly."

Ken is stunned as he makes another move on the board.

"You talked to Mariah?" He asks, filled with curiosity.

"Yeah, we talked."

"About what?" he inquires.

Victoria giggles before moving her next piece.

"Girl talk," she responds.

"What does that mean?"

"Well, you'd have to be a girl to understand," Victoria responds, awaiting Ken's next move. "Are you going to move or what?"

Ken is still stunned as he quickly makes a move. Victoria moves again quickly and can tell Ken is clearly off his game when Mariah's name comes up.

"I will say this, she told me you've been avoiding her for a couple of weeks. I think she misses you," she says while he moves his next piece.

"She said that?" Ken inquires as Victoria moves her piece once again.

"She didn't say it like that, but I can tell she really cares," Victoria answers. "That's check by the way."

Ken looks at the board and blocks her check, as Victoria quickly moves once again.

"So, what's the deal between you two? It's like you're both are a couple, but not a couple," she replies as Ken makes a move on the board.

"It's complicated," Ken responds with a chuckle. "I made up the word to describe it. Flirtationship."

Victoria looks at Ken strangely before moving her next

piece.

"Please explain that one," she says. "Check."

Ken sighs as he makes a move to block Victoria once again.

"It's basically a lot of flirting, but nothing going on," Ken explains. "She's just strange."

"I could tell. She's very protective of you," Victoria responds before moving her next piece. "Check again."

"Don't believe the hype, trust me," Ken responds as he blocks his friend's chess move. "It's all an act just to mess with my head. There's nothing there."

Victoria smiles as quickly moves her queen on the board once again.

"That's checkmate," Victoria replies, stunning Ken, who cautiously looks at the board trying to see if there is a way out. "And trust me, I'm a female. I know when there's something there or not. There's something there, you just need to figure out a way to make it work. New game?"

Ken is still stunned as he nods his head, agreeing to the rematch. As he watches his friend set up the chessboard, he notices something and smiles.

"Hey, why are you always playing as white?" He asks with a smirk. "Maybe I wanna be first for once."

"Hey, I'm always white because I'm white," Victoria responds with a smile. "And you're always black because... well, you know."

Ken laughs as he nods his head with approval.

"Well, I can't argue there," he says as she puts back on her headphones and starts bobbing her head to the music once more.

"What is that you're listening to?" Ken asks as Victoria makes her first move on the board.

"Ace of Base," she replies to a confused Ken.

"Ace of what?"

"Ace of Base. The Sign. Here, check it out," she says as she hands Ken her headphones.

He puts them on and bobs his head as well before moving his first piece.

"Hey, this kinda tight," he responds. "Definitely something the folks in Kansas would bump."

"Yeah, they're pretty cool," she responds as she makes her second move of the game.

The two friends continue their chess game laughing and joking with each other as the lunch period continues. Ken wins the second game easily as he's much more focused this time.

Victoria and Ken are walking out of class later that day making their way to the front gate of the school. Mariah is sitting with a couple of her friends when she notices the two. Ken notices her as well as he nods his head to her.

"Well, this has been a fun day," Victoria responds with a smile. "I finally beat you in chess, and it only took me a couple of weeks to do so."

"You got lucky," Ken responds with a smirk.

"No, I distracted you with your, what did you call her again? Oh, your flirtationship," a smug Victoria responds, embarrassing Ken. "Any woman who can make a chess master such as yourself lose to a novice like me is more than a flirtationship. She's special to you. Don't let that go."

Ken sighs and nods his head with understanding as Mariah finally makes her way towards them.

"Hey, Vikki," she says as she hugs Victoria. "How's it been going?"

"It's been going well, I have to say," she responds with a smile. "Well, let me get out of here before I miss my bus. I'll see you both tomorrow."

Mariah nods her head with a smile as Victoria heads off towards the bus stop. Ken looks at Mariah suspiciously, trying to figure out her newfound respect for Mariah.

"Vikki?" He responds as Mariah looks at him, confused.

"What?"

"I'm tryin' to figure out how you went from Militant Mariah when it came towards Victoria to 'Vikki?' Like y'all are best friends now," Ken points out.

"She's not that bad, I'll admit," Mariah responds. "I mean, come on, Ken. I haven't dealt with many white folks in my life. They're all the same to me, for real. I didn't like you being mad at me over this, so I decided to meet up with her and see what is it that got you all crazy over her."

"I'm not crazy over her," Ken responds as he and Mariah start walking towards the bus stop. "I was just tryin' to help her adjust here. That's all."

"I don't know. I mean you've been bootin' up at me for the last couple of weeks over her," Mariah points out. "You ain't never act like that to me before. I'll admit, she ain't that bad. A lot different than I imagined."

"She's a person, just like you and me," Ken responds as they both take a seat at an empty bench.

"Well, she's definitely like you, I'll give you that," Mariah says with a giggle. "That proper tone sounded just like you did when you first got here."

Ken chuckles as Mariah shakes her head with a grin.

"Look, I wanna say sorry for that," she responds. "Maybe I was a little jealous and got caught up. Don't get me wrong, I still have strong feelings about this whole racial thing, but after talkin' to the girl, I can see why you're down with her."

Ken nods his head with acceptance, appreciating Mariah's apology.

"I know I come from a different world than you're used to. I had to adjust the way I think," Ken responds. "Being an army brat does that to you. Always having to adapt. I'd like to think I keep some of the good in me though. Some things that no matter where I'm at, it remains consistent. I'm just trying to be good in a world filled with bad, you know."

Mariah nods her head as the two friends sit silently together on the bench. After a few moments, Ken looks towards Mariah with a smirk on his face.

"So, she told me you two had a little girl talk," he says. "Care to enlighten me on what y'all discussed?"

Mariah bursts into laughter shaking her head in denial. Ken continues to try and get it out of her, but Mariah keeps quiet about her and Victoria's discussion. Ken guesses that in that discussion, Mariah admitted some things to Victoria about how she felt about him, but was unable to get his friend to admit that much.

The next school day, Ken walks into Mr. Jenkins's class and daps off Walter, who is setting up a chessboard.

"What's up, dude?" Ken says as he looks around the classroom. "Victoria made it up yet?"

"Nah, I haven't seen her," Walter responds. "She's in

my Algebra class normally, and she wasn't there either. She probably called out sick or something."

Ken thinks for a moment before nodding his head.

"Alright. Well, who you 'bout to play right now?" he asks.

"Oh, you want some of this?" Walter responds with a smirk. "Step up to the plate if you wanna get this ass whoopin'."

"Nah, neph. You must got me confused with someone else. Let's run," Ken responds as he takes a seat across from Walter.

The two start a competitive game that goes back and forth throughout with Ken seeking his first win against the more skillful Walter.

Later in drafting class, Ken, Reggie, and the other students are all laughing and talking with each other when Mr. Scalise enters the classroom. Ken looks over and can tell his teacher was upset.

"Yo, Mr. Scalise. Is everythin' cool," he asks, getting his teacher's attention.

Mr. Scalise sighs before addressing the class.

"Everyone, let me have your attention," he says, quieting the students down. "I just wanted to let everyone know that Victoria will no longer attend school here."

Everyone in the class is stunned, including Ken who is speechless.

"Yesterday after school, there was an altercation on the city bus. Apparently, she accidentally stepped on another female's shoe, and the female cut her face over it," Mr. Scalise says almost in anger. "Her parents reported the incident to the school and said she will not return."

His tone seemed like he was angry at the class, who are all black teens, for the attack. After the announcement, he takes a seat behind his desk as the class all looks around at each other, still trying to process the news. Ken fights to keep his emotions in check as Reggie looks at him and can tell he's struggling.

"Yo, I'm sorry, Ken," he says, trying to comfort his friend. "I know y'all were cool and shit. That's messed up, for real."

Ken slowly nods his head as he's still having a hard

time processing what happened.

As class ends for the day, Ken walks out of the school gate, still in a daze. Nothing made sense to him at that moment. Just thinking about the day prior, not knowing it would be the last time he would see her depresses him. Mariah is sitting outside of the gate, waiting for him. She notices the look on his face as soon as she approaches him.

"Hey, how you doin'?" she asks as the two walk off towards the side of the front building, away from the crowds.

"You heard about Victoria?" He somberly asks.

Mariah nods her head, saddened by the incident as well.

"I heard it was Venus and her bunch that did it," Mariah responds.

"Venus?"

"Yeah. That bitch always was one for startin' shit. She ain't nothin' but a coward though," Mariah responds. "Me and her got into it in the sixth grade. She talked all that noise, but when I got with her, she tried to sucker punch me in front of her friends. I beat that bitch's ass so bad that day. She was lucky the teachers stopped me, or I'd still be beatin' her ass."

"How could this happen though?" Ken says, seeking answers. "I mean what would cause someone to be so cruel? Victoria wasn't one to start trouble, you know that. She spent most of her time here scared to death, so I know she wouldn't have approached Venus or anyone else like that."

Mariah sighs as she tries to calm her friend down.

"Ken, I can bet that Victoria didn't do anything wrong," she replies. "I told you how it is out here. If she was black, probably nothin' would have happened. Like I said, Venus is a coward. Being that it was a white girl though, she knew she could do what she wanted to that poor girl."

Ken takes a deep breath trying to control his emotions. Mariah's explanation wasn't satisfying his rage.

"I'm fuckin' sick and tired of this shit!" He exclaims, causing Mariah to get nervous. "All this shit doesn't make sense! What kind of a world do we live in where shit like this happens?!"

"Ken, calm down," Mariah says, trying to get him to focus. "Look at me! I said look at me!"

Ken's eyes slowly connect with hers as Mariah tries to explain the truth of the situation to him.

"We are in New Orleans," she replies. "Is it right? No, it's not, but it is what it is. A friend of mine, Sharice, got jumped on Canal street a week ago 'cause she was wearin' her school uniform. A bunch of Fortier bitches she didn't even know attacked her. She wasn't about that life. She didn't deserve that. None of us do, just like Victoria didn't. It is what it is though. It's always been like that out here, and it's never gonna change. Never. It pisses me off Victoria went through that, it really does, but this is what life is like down here. It ain't easy, Ken, but it is what it is."

Ken shakes his head in denial, refusing to accept his friend's words. He backs away from her slightly, but she walks back up to him and hugs him, trying to remove the rage that fills his heart. Initially, he rejects her hug, trying to distance himself from her, but Mariah refuses to loosen her grip. Ken eventually gives into her as tears start falling from his eyes. He can no longer fight his emotions as the embrace from his close friend does the job and removes the rage from his heart. All that remains is sadness as losing his friend for whatever reason weighs heavy in his heart.

The following weekend, Ken walks into his room with a bag in his hand from the music store. He takes a seat on his bed and takes out an Ace of Base CD he's purchased. He checks out the cover as a small smirk enters his face reminiscing about Victoria. After checking out the CD, he puts on 'The Sign,' the song that he and his friend once shared. He chuckles to himself, thinking how she would always bob her head when playing this song. He wanted to feel the song so that he would never forget about her and the tragic way their friendship ended. He takes out his songbook and lists her name and the song in it to make their bond official, ensuring he would always remember her. He repeats the song before lying down in his bed. In the back of his head, he hopes that the two will cross paths once again. He knows she's still out there, and maybe one day soon they would meet again.

Chapter 6

French Summer (Aaliyah - Street Thing) - 1995

It's the final day school of Ken and Mariah's eleventh-grade year. The two are sitting at a bus stop amongst a group of other students at the corner of the school talking with each other as the summer has officially started. Both have gotten taller and have changed their appearance with the updated times. Ken has gone back to his old box, high top fade haircut, ditching the old curl style, and Mariah is sporting her new short hair finger wave do. As the first bus arrives, the students all rush the bus, eager to get their summer vacation started. After a few pushes and shoves, Mariah nods to Ken as they both back away from the crowd. The bus is almost filled to capacity as the two friends take a seat once again.

"People do not play when it comes to the summer," Mariah says as the bus pulls off.

"For real! I thought it was gonna be another riot like we had when they canceled that dance in ninth grade," Ken says, causing Mariah to laugh.

"I remember that shit. You was scared like mug," she says with a smirk.

"Yeah, whatever. So what you got goin' this summer?" Ken asks, changing the subject.

"I don't know. I mean, not all of us can go to, where was it again? Tulsa," Mariah asks flippantly.

"Tallulah," Ken corrects.

"Right. Sounds like some raggedy-ass town in Mississippi," Mariah mocks 'cause she knows it pushes Ken's buttons. "I mean, what are you even gonna do in that small ass town."

"Enjoy some peace and quiet," Ken responds. "Don't have to look over my shoulder every five minutes like I do here. It's gonna be wonderful."

"Fool, please. I know why you runnin' your ass out there. You talk shit about my city, but living here carries a rep," Mariah points out. "You go to them lil' ass cites saying you from the N.O., and all the girls probably drop they draws for ya. Them women see the same dudes out there every day, so when something new runs though there, they be all up on it. Tell me I'm lying. You ain't slick."

Ken chuckles to himself as the thought has crossed his mind. His cousin, Tiara, who lives in Tallulah, is his hook up. She was a few years younger than him, but her spot on the local cheerleading team meant she was in contact with some of the finest females the town had to offer. She always made it a point to bring him around to every event to show him off.

"Why you worried about what I'm doing?" Ken responds. "What you need to do is worry about Robert."

"You soundin' real jealous right now," Mariah says with a smirk.

"Me jealous?! Of Robert?! Girl, you trippin'," Ken responds. "Why I gotta be jealous of some slugged up, pompadour hair having, reading at a third-grade level ass dude for?"

"Baby, I know you not talkin' after last year's phone girlfriend," Mariah points out. "How you gonna clown Rob when you was datin' Melanie, a lil' girl you ain't never met?"

Ken had to give her that one. She was referring to a young girl his cousin Denard was dating at the time. One day while spending the night over by his cousin's house, Denard was chatting on the phone when he suddenly put the phone down and went to sleep. A curious Ken picked up the phone and sparked a conversation with Melanie, who had no idea Denard went to sleep on her and hit it off with her. The next day, he had told Denard about it, and his cousin was fine with him getting with Melanie saying he was tired of her anyway. He spent the next few months talking with Melanie over the phone and even exchanged pictures with each other via mail, but the two never actually met in person. Eventually, their phone relationship fell apart. Mariah always gave Ken a hard time over the relationship calling it the 'funniest thing ever.' Ken never had a comeback for that.

"See, that was a low blow," Ken responds, lowering his head in shame.

"You know I gotta put you in check when you come for my boo," Mariah says before playfully punching him in the arm.

As they wait for the bus, Shona and Denise, two classmates of theirs, walk over and join them at the bus stop. Shona was tall, lanky, and dark-skinned. She met Ken through Mariah, who is her one of her closest friends. He wasn't her biggest fan as she would gossip about any and everyone. She was the messy, loud type that he wasn't interested in involving himself with. Denise, however, was the exact opposite of what Shona was. She was around average height and quiet. He met her in tenth grade in biology class, and the two had become cool with each other since then. Outside of Mariah, she's the closest female he would interact with on a day to day basis.

"Hey, y'all. Did you hear about Moe?" Shona says, living up to her gossipy nature. "They said he got shot in the projects last night. Natalya is a mess over it."

"Hey, girl. Yeah, I heard about it," Mariah says. "They had to pull Natalya outta class early. I can't believe that shit."

"I know, right? Didn't Toon use to run with him?" Shona asks Ken, who nods his head.

"Yeah, he did," Ken responds. "Well, he did until he got picked up for that armed robbery charge a few months ago."

Shona nods her head as she takes a seat next to Mariah. Denise sits next to Ken as the classmates change the subject. They start laughing and conversing with each other, looking forward to a summer without school.

A week later, Ken is in Tallulah sitting at the lounge area next to the concession stand of a local skating rink. The rink is packed with teens who are either skating on the floor, hanging out in the concession area, or playing the few available arcade games. The lounge area had several TVs playing the NBA Finals game between the Magic and the Rockets. Ken has his Orlando Magic shirt and hat on watching as Orlando's Nick Anderson walks to the free-throw line after being fouled. He's on the edge of his seat but is irritated when Anderson missed both free throws at the waning moments of the game.

"Son of a bitch," he says to himself as he watches Houston get the ball back and score.

The game is over several minutes later as Ken, and several others walk off at the conclusion. His cousin, Tiara, notices him and skates over.

"Why are you looking like that?" She asks.

"Stupid Magic lost the freaking game," Ken responds, being more careful with his words than he normally would.

Ken would normally change his tone and dialect depending on who he was dealing with. He was very conscious about using slang he learned in New Orleans to anyone else. Even his cousin didn't get the full New Orleans from him. She laughed at him getting upset over a basketball game. He looked at the two pigtails that she had flowing down to her shoulders, pondering how much trouble would he get into if he yanked her down by them. He and Tiara were the two oldest cousins on his mother's side and would bump heads every so often. Before Ken could react, Tiara stops him with a smirk on her face, meaning she had some interesting news regarding a hook up for him.

"Who are we looking at?" Ken suspiciously asks.

"Girl with the all-black on and the sparkling skates standing next to the rink," Tiara points out.

Ken takes a look over towards the rink side when he notices who his cousin was referring to. He was fairly impressed with the selection, even though she was a little shorter than he would like.

"What's her name?" He asks.

"Monica."

"You told her about me?" Ken asks as Tiara nods her head. "And? What did she say?"

"She thinks you're cute and wouldn't mind meeting you," Tiara responds. "I can walk you over and introduce you if you want?"

"Alright. Let me go get me something to drink real fast, and I'll meet up with you," Ken responds.

Tiara nods her head and skates off as Ken walks over to the concession stand and places his order. As he waits for his drink, he notices three cute females skating by smiling at him. Ken smiles as his confidence level is at a high. One of the females skates over and stands next to him, greeting him with a smile.

"Hey."

"Hey," Ken replies with a smile of his own.

"Aren't you Tiara's cousin? Ken?" She asks.

"Yeah, that's me," Ken responds as his drink arrives.

"And you are?"

"Alisha," she answers.

Ken checks her out and likes what he sees. He notices her hair, which is in a ponytail, and her beautiful smile. She had a nice, coke bottle-shaped body with smooth caramel skin. After taking her in, Ken smiles and starts to do his best to impress her.

"So, Ms. Alisha, how's your night going?" He asked in his more New Orleans dialect.

"It's fine. I was wondering if we can talk a little," Alisha says nervously.

"Sure," Ken replies with a smile as he leads her over to an unoccupied table.

Ken is usually the nervous one in conversations like this, but Alisha's nervousness has him feeling in control for the first time in a while. The two sit down as Ken leads the conversation.

As the night goes on, Alisha and Ken have become comfortable with each other as she's laughing at several things he tells her. The skating rink is closing down as people start to file out of the building. Ken rises from his chair once he notices everything is shutting down.

"Damn, that time flew by," he says as Alisha rises from her chair as well.

"It always does when you're having a good time," she responds with a smirk.

There is an awkward silence between the two since both of them have timid personalities. Alisha finally manages to break the silence.

"Hey, so I was wondering... I... well... can I get your number?" She asks with a hint of embarrassment.

"Um... sure, I guess," Ken replies.

Alisha goes into her purse and hands him some paper and a pen when Ken realizes he doesn't know his aunt's number.

"Excuse me one second," he says before hurrying off to find Tiara.

He's finally able to locate her just inside the entrance to the rink.

"Hey, what's your phone number?" He asks a confused Tiara.

"What's my number? How about where in the hell were you?" Tiara responds. "I had my girl Monica waiting there all night for you!"

"Just write down your number, damn!" Ken exclaims, handing her the paper and pen Alisha had given him.

Tiara sighs with an attitude as she writes down the number and hands it back to Ken. He quickly rushes back over to Alisha and hands her the paper.

"Thanks," she says with a grin. "Well, I guess I better go. I'm sure my ride is out there waiting on me, and I still need to go turn in my skates."

"Oh, my bad, I didn't mean to keep you," Ken responds. "Hope to hear from you soon."

Alisha smiles once more before making her way over to the turn-in area. Ken gives a fist pump just as Tiara approaches him with her arms folded.

"Who did you give my number to?" She asks with an attitude.

"Some girl named Alisha. You know her?" Ken asks.

Tiara cringes before nodding her head.

"Alisha? Why are you fooling with that girl?" Tiara

responds.

"Why not?"

"You do realize she's in the ninth grade, right?" Tiara points out. "She's the same age as you but three grades behind. Did you even think about that?"

Ken is stunned as their grades never came up in their discussion.

"I... I didn't know," Ken admits. "Okay, she's a little slow, so what? It's not like I'm going to marry her or something."

"Yeah, see the thing is she's not three grades behind because she's slow. At least I don't think it is. No, the reason is she had a baby in eighth grade and missed a whole lot of time in class. She just started going back to school not too long ago," Tiara responds, shocking Ken again.

"A baby? Are you serious?" Ken asks.

"Yes, I am. You're wasting all your time messing with her when my girl Monica, who is a straight-A student I might add, was interested in you," she quips.

"What do you mean *was* interested?"

"Well, when you stood her up, she didn't want to be bothered with you anymore," Tiara responds to a disappointed Ken. "Can't believe you gave that hussie my number."

Tiara continues to berate Ken as the two cousins make their way outside of the skating rink, looking for their ride.

The next day, Ken is in his auntie's den watching TV when Tiara walks in with the cordless phone in her hand.

"It's for you," she says with a hint of attitude.

"Who is it?" Ken asks.

"Who do you think?"

Ken nods his head as he takes the phone from his cousin and walks outside to the porch area to take the call.

"Hello?"

"Hey, Ken. It's Alisha," she says.

"Hey, what's up?" Ken replies, trying to not sound too interested.

"Nothing much. Just wanted to check and see what you're up to."

Ken sighs. After what he's learned, he's not too sure

he wants to deal with Alisha. Her having a child at such a young age told him all he needed to know about her. The fact that the child never came up during their conversation was also telling.

"I'm cool. Listen, I got something to ask you, and I want you to be real with me," Ken says with a hint of seriousness in his voice. "I'm hearing some things about you, and I don't know how I feel about it."

"Let me guess, your cousin told you about my baby," Alisha responds, causing Ken to look on with disappointment.

"Pretty much," Ken responds. "Why didn't you say something when we met last night?"

"Let's be real, Ken. You know how hard it is to get a guy to talk to you when you lead with 'oh, by the way, I have a kid,'" Alisha answers. "This whole town knows about it, and I'm treated like shit because of it. Everybody has their own opinion about it, and that's fine. I chose to keep my son, and I would choose him again if I had to."

Ken softens his stance slightly, not thinking how much of an outsider her situation would make her feel. It reminded him of his first year back to New Orleans, and how he felt.

"Yeah, I... I guess that never crossed my mind," he responds.

"So, I guess you don't want to be bothered with me now?" Alisha asks.

Ken thinks for a moment because he has an out if he wanted. All he has to say is 'no,' and he would never have to deal with her anymore. He was empathetic to her situation and knew how it felt to be alone.

"Nah, I'm cool. I'm cool," Ken replies. "Just caught me off guard, that's all. Anything else you wanna tell me? Like you were born a dude or somethin'?"

Alisha laughs as the two continue their conversation with each other.

Several weeks later, Ken and Alisha are sitting outside of Ken's aunt's house on the porch enjoying the slight summer breeze as Ken gazes at the stars. The neighborhood is rather quiet, with only the sounds of crickets heard throughout the area. The two have been dating throughout the past couple of weeks and have become attached. They've been on several dates hanging with others, but they mostly enjoyed the time they had alone with each other. Alisha notices how enamored her boyfriend is with the stars.

"What are you thinking about like that?" She asks, interrupting his gaze.

"Huh? Oh, it's nothing," Ken replies before turning his attention back towards the sky. "I'm just admiring the stars, that's all. Don't get to see that where I'm at anymore."

"I don't get it," a confused Alisha replies before moving in closer to her friend and gazing at the stars with him. "It's just stars and stuff. What's the big deal?"

"You can't see the stars in the city," Ken points out. "One of the things I always loved about coming out here is that I don't have to be on my guard all the time. It's nice and quiet. I can hear myself think for a while. I can sit back and enjoy the beauty the world has to offer. It's almost poetic."

Alisha chuckles as Ken's words impress her.

"I can see someone got an A in English class," she jokes.

"It wasn't all that hard to get an A out there, trust me," Ken quips, causing Alisha to laugh. After a few moments, the couple both enjoy the atmosphere once again.

"I mean, listen to it out here," Ken points out. "All the crickets and shit. Baby, you don't know how good you have it out here."

"Grass is always greener, I guess," Alisha responds as Ken nods his head.

"Maybe," he says.

After a few moments, Alisha turns to Ken with a smile on her face.

"Look, I... I got a gift for you. Well, us a gift," she says as she goes into her book bag.

"A gift?"

"Yeah, I hope you like it," Alisha responds as she pulls out a gift bag and hands it to Ken. "Go ahead. Open it."

"Wow, I don't know what to say," Ken says as he opens the bag.

The gift was two small plush teddy bears. One was a

boy teddy bear, and the other was a girl. Ken looks confused as Alisha has a hint of excitement in her eyes.

"Teddy bears?" Ken asks.

"Yeah! The girl one is for you and the boy one is for me," Alisha says as she takes the boy bear.

"Why am I getting the girl one?" a confused Ken asks.

"Don't you see?" Alisha responds. "She's me! Anywhere you go, even when you go home, she'll always be with you. Same with him to me."

Ken finally catches on as he smiles. Alisha looks on with disappointment.

"You don't like it, do you?" She asks.

"Huh? No, I love it! It's just... I hate having to be explained about it," Ken replies. "I should have picked up on it."

"It's a girl gift. I didn't expect you to get it," Alisha says with a chuckle. "I think I'll call my bear Ken Junior. KJ for short."

"Really? I was thinking about naming mine Mary J. Bear," Ken replies, much to Alisha's displeasure.

"Mary J. Huh?" She responds with an attitude. "See,

you trying to start some mess."

"Nah, I'm not trying to start anything," Ken fires back. "You name your bear whatever you want, and I'll name mine whatever I want."

"Oh, yeah?" Alisha responds before folding her arms.

Ken nods his head confidently before Alisha attempts to snatch the bear back from him. She's unable to as Ken jumps up from the porch running into the lawn, followed closely by Alisha. She tackles him to the ground as the two wrestles over the new bear. After several moments, the two start laughing as they sit up from the ground breathing heavily from their activity.

"Look at you. Got me all down here in the grass," Alisha says, trying to catch her breath.

"It's your own fault," Ken points out.

"The bear is named Alisha, and you better call her that!" Alisha snaps back.

"No Mary J. Bear?" Ken playfully responds.

Alisha frowns at him before Ken gives in and gives her was she wants.

"Fine. Lil' Alisha it is," he says with a smirk.

Alisha nods her head with approval as she looks at her watch. She gets up from the ground and dusts herself off as best she can.

"And with that, let me get out of here," she says.

Ken quickly gets up and dusts himself off as well.

"Why you runnin' off?" He asks.

"Look at the time. If I don't get home, my dad will kill me and you, and not necessarily in that order," Alisha responds.

"Good point," Ken says as Alisha collects her things.

Alisha is about to walk off when Ken pulls her back.

"You gonna call me?" He asks.

"I'll sneak the phone up in my room," Alisha answers with a smirk. "How late are you gonna be up?"

"Until you call me."

"Damn, it must be nice to be able to talk on the phone whenever you want," Alisha responds.

"One of the many benefits of being away from home," Ken says with a sly grin. "So when you gonna call me?"

"When I call."

"And what am I supposed to do from now until then,"

Ken flirts.

Alisha smiles as she begins walking away.

"Lil Alisha will keep you company. Think about me until then," she says as she makes her way down the street.

Ken watches her for as far as he can see before heading back onto the porch. He takes a seat and looks over Lil' Alisha. He chuckles to himself as he sits the bear next to him and starts gazing at the stars once more.

A month later, Ken and Alisha are back at the skating rink. They are in a secluded area towards the back where the lights are dim, and several couples are there, hand in hand with each other. They are sitting on a bench with a full view of the back end of the rink. Alisha notices Ken's mood isn't what it normally is.

"Hey, you alright?" She inquires.

"Yeah, I... I guess it just hit me that this is our last week together," he admits.

"You just thinking about that?" Alisha asks.

"Yeah. I mean, I just got so caught up in the moment that I didn't think about it until now," Ken confesses.

Alisha nods her head with understanding before lying her head on Ken's shoulder.

"Truth be told, I thought about it a couple of weeks back," she says. "I was like here I am, finally found me a cute guy to hang with, and he's gonna be back at home at the end of summer. Just temporary."

"You've been thinking about this for a couple of weeks?" Ken asks.

"Yep."

"How come you never mentioned it?" He asks.

"I don't know. Would it have mattered?" She replies.

"I guess not," Ken replies with a look of sadness in his eyes. "I guess it's cool to know I'm not the only one thinking like this."

"Ken, this has been the best summer of my life," Alisha responds with her eyes watering. "I always knew you'd be going back home and that this wouldn't last. I figured I had two options. I could stress on it and spend the rest of our time together depressed, or I can live every moment as if it was our last together."

Ken sighs as he knew she is right about living for the

moment.

"Shit, I guess I never thought about it like that," he says.

"I love you, Ken," Alisha says as she gazes into his eyes. "I don't want to see you go, but we can still be together when you leave. It'll be hard, but we can make it work."

"Make it work? How?" A confused Ken responds.

"We can write and talk on the phone, you know," Alisha says, trying to pitch the idea to Ken. "You're always saying you're down here visiting, right? We could make this work. I don't know, maybe I can visit you. See what the big city has to offer."

Ken chuckles as he tries to bring his girlfriend back to reality.

"Now you know good and damn well your pops ain't gonna allow that," he says.

"You forget, I'm a daddy's girl," she reminds him. "I get what I want when I want."

Ken doesn't buy into her thoughts on visiting him. He let the comment go as Alisha was looking at any way to keep the connection between them going. He never considered a long-distance relationship with her because he didn't think it would work. Still, looking in her eyes, he could tell she was serious with wanting to keep the relationship going. Before he could respond, the DJ starts playing Aaliyah's *Street Thing*. The lights dim throughout the entire rink, making it almost completely dark where both Ken and Alisha are located. Couples cuddle up on the skating floor and throughout the rink with Ken and Alisha also cuddling up.

"So, can you stay faithful?" Ken asks.

"Hell yeah. Can you?" she asks back.

Ken hesitates as Alisha looks at him with an attitude. He bursts into laughter after seeing her response.

"Damn, girl. You should have seen your face," he says.

"Don't play with me!" Alisha fires back. "You was about to have me acting a fool in this place."

"Come on, girl. You know you my one and only. I'm not tryin' to be with anyone else," a smooth-talking Ken responds.

Alisha smiles as she quickly pulls Ken down, forcing

him to lie his head on her lap.

"Hey!" Ken says with confusion.

"Something to make sure you don't forget about me when you're back home," Alisha states before moving in and giving Ken his first kiss much to his surprise.

They share the passionate kiss that lasts for several moments. Ken slowly rises from Alisha's lap afterward taken aback with what just happened.

"Where did that come from?" He asks.

"I don't know. Was it alright?" Alisha asks.

"Well, there's only one way to really tell if it's alright or not," Ken says before quickly moving in and kissing Alisha once more.

As Aaliyah's song filled the rink, Ken and Alisha continue their passionate make-out session. After the song ends, the light brightens once again, causing the couple to back away from each other, both with smiles on their faces.

"Who would have known that you were such a great kisser," Alisha says with a smirk.

"Well, I don't know about all that, but I do know that was a moment I will never forget," Ken says.

"There's another moment I'd like to give you if you're up for it," Alisha responds, piquing her boyfriend's interest. "My parents are going out of town this weekend. One last trip before the summer ends. They are going to visit my grandparents in Biloxi. I convinced them to let me stay home."

Ken catches on to what she is asking.

"I see," he says while he considers her proposal. "What about the baby?"

"Anthony is going with them," Alisha responds. "I'll be all alone, and would love to have some company."

A hint of nervousness fills Ken as he never expected the offer he was given. He didn't know if he was ready for sex. Some of his friends, including Mariah, were already sexually active, but he was unsure if he wanted to join the others.

"So, what do you think?" Alisha asks.

"I... I don't know what to think," Ken responds.

"Tell you what, how about we enjoy the night. In a couple of days, you come by my spot, and what happens, happens," Alisha offers.

Ken thinks for a moment before slowly nodding his head with agreement.

"Alright, I'm with that," he says.

He's about to rise from the bench when Alisha suddenly pulls him back down.

"Where do you think you going?" she asks before surprising him with a kiss once again.

The two continued to kiss even though the lights have returned to their normal state. Alisha wants her on Ken's mind, which is why she chose to be aggressive with him. The more she turns him on, the more likely he'd decide to hook up with her later that week. Ken has never had this type of affection prior, so his decision-making skills are not at their peak for the moment.

Later that night, Ken is lying in bed thinking about his options. He didn't want to seem scared to have sex, but he wasn't sure if he was ready. STDs and pregnancy are just a few of his things that crossed his mind while trying to come up with a decision. One thing he knew for certain is that his first kiss deserved a spot in his songbook. He rolls over to the side of the bed and pulls out his songbook from his backpack. He opens it up and lists 'Street Thing' by Aaliyah on his list of songs. After a few moments, he looks towards Lil Alisha with a smirk on his face.

"What you lookin' at?" he says to the bear before putting his songbook back into his book sack.

He takes a look at the bear once more, and just as Alisha had planned all along, it reminds him of her. He thinks back to their make-out session from earlier and smiles. All his concerns fly out the window as he makes a decision that would forever change his life. He cuts off the lamp and calls it a night. He glances at Lil' Alisha with a smirk on his face before turning over to go to sleep.

The following Saturday, Alisha opens her front door to a smiling Ken. Her face lights up as she welcomes him into her home. As Ken makes his way through the house, he's impressed as it was a lot better than Alisha had let on. She wastes no time trying to get what she wanted as she led him to her bedroom. Ken is nervous as he looks around her room.

"This… this is nice," he says as Alisha kicks off her flip flops.

"It is what it is," she says as she approaches him.

As she moves in close, Ken is visually nervous. She notices how uneasy he seems as she tries to calm him down.

"Hey, just relax," she says. "Don't stress. I got this."

She walks over and kisses him passionately as she works him over towards the bed. She slightly pushes him on the bed and mounts him with a smirk on her face. She removes her shirt to reveal her bra, and it was at this moment when it became real for Ken. He knew there was no turning back if things went any further. Alisha, for her part, was very relaxed as she slowly removes Ken's shirt. She runs her fingers down his chest and to his stomach, causing him to giggle.

"Wow, you're so ticklish," she says with a sinister grin. "Let's see if I can make you smile some more."

Alisha runs her fingers down Ken's sides this time, causing Ken to laugh loudly. He tries to stop her, but she is relentless. After a few moments, he's forced to toss her to the side and mount her while securing her hands over her head, leaving her helpless. She smiles as it was the position she wanted to be in the most.

"That's more like it," she says. "Go ahead. Do what you feel. Touch me."

Ken does as commanded as he continues to secure her wrists with one hand while running his hands down her body with the other causing her to close her eyes. Alisha would react to certain spots Ken would touch, which would cause her to either giggle or slightly moan. Just as he's about to reach for her breasts, he stops. He catches a glance of the baby crib in her room from the corner of his eyes, which is what causes him to hesitate. Alisha opens her eyes and can see the concern in her boyfriend's eyes.

"Ken? What's the matter?" She asks.

"I... I... I can't do this," he responds as he releases his grasp from her wrists and rises. "I'm... I'm sorry."

Ken dismounts her and looks for his shirt on the side of the bed as a disappointed Alisha rises from the bed as well.

"Ken, calm down," she says as he puts on his shirt.

"Just... can we talk for a second? Please?"

After putting on his shirt, Ken pauses for a moment, sitting on the edge of her bed. Alisha scoots over and hugs him from behind, trying to calm his mind.

"Please don't leave," she says before kissing him on his neck.

Ken shakes his head as he rejects her affection and rises from the bed.

"I can't, Lisha. I just can't," he says before walking out of the bedroom and out of her house.

Alisha is devastated with the rejection as tears fill her eyes. She puts back on her shirt and lies back in the bed, disappointed things didn't work out the way she had hoped.

A week later, summer vacation in Tallulah is over as Ken is packing his things into his dad's car. He's taking one final look to make sure he has everything when he notices Alisha on the curb looking at him. He looks around before approaching her. He sees the sadness in her eyes. After the incident at her home, they hadn't spoken. He was embarrassed about what happened and wouldn't take her calls. When she would stop by, he would tell Tiara to tell her that he wasn't there. Now, in their final moments together, Ken regrets not speaking with her.

"Hey," she says.

"Hey," he responds as they mimic their first words to each other. "What's goin' on?"

"Just came to see you off," Alisha replies. "I... I didn't know if it was right or not, but-"

"It's fine," a reassuring Ken responds. "Look, about last week. I just... I'm so sorry about what happened. I was just... It's..."

Ken is at a loss for words as Alisha calms him down.

"I know, Ken. It's fine, really," she says. "It's my fault too. I shouldn't have put you in that situation until you were ready. With you going home, I didn't know the next time we would see each other, and I wanted to make sure you wouldn't forget me."

Ken chuckles as he looks at his girl.

"Trust me, there is no possible way I will ever forget you. You forget, I got Lil' Alisha," he says, causing Alisha to giggle.

She wipes a few tears from her face before handing Ken a note.

"It has my address on it. I hope you will still mail me when you get back to N.O.," she says.

Ken takes the note and nods his head in agreement.

"Of course I will," he says before his father calls out to him ready to go.

He takes a look at Alisha, who is on the brink of tears. The two share a hug with each other. After a few moments, Alisha backs away, taking one last look at Ken before walking off down the street. Ken sighs before jumping in the car with his parents as he buckles his seat belt in the back seat. As the car pulls off, it goes towards the opposite direction from which Alisha had gone. Ken's eyes water as well, but he hides it to keep his thoughts to himself. He puts on his headphones and loads Aaliyah's CD into his Discman, which he got for his birthday. He selects the 'Street Thing' song from the tracklist and nestles his head to the side door in preparation for the long drive back to New Orleans.

A little under four hours later, Ken and his sister are unloading the car and heading into the house as they stretch their legs. As Ken drops off his book sack, the house phone suddenly rings. He quickly answers the phone.

"Hello."

"Welcome back, Kansas," Mariah says, confusing Ken.

"Jesus Christ, what are you posted outside my house or something?" Ken asks. "I literally just walked into the front door."

"Boy, please. I know where you are at all times," Mariah fires back. "I know when you've been naughty and nice too, baby. I'm feelin' a naughty vibe coming from you."

Ken chuckles as he quickly makes his way to his room and closes the door.

"All I'll say is I had a nice summer," Ken says with a smirk before plopping on his bed.

"Please, ain't nothin' to do in Tallulah, Mississippi," Mariah fires back.

"It's Louisiana, thank you very much," Ken corrects.

"And, baby, let me tell you 'bout the summer of ninety-five."

"Before you go into your boring summer, I was calling to see if you heard about Walter?" Mariah says, interrupting her friend.

"Walter? Which Walter?" Ken inquires.

"The one you were in the chess club with," she answers, causing Ken to frown.

"I wasn't in a chess club!" Ken fires back. "How many times I gotta tell you-"

"My bad, damn. Look, about a week ago, Walter was leaving from a party and was standing at the bus stop about to go home when somebody shot him," Mariah responds, stunning Ken.

"He... he got shot?" Ken replies. "Is he okay?"

"He's dead," Mariah responds, breaking the news to Ken.

Sadness enters his face as the news sucks the life out of Ken. Walter had just graduated at the end of the school year. They weren't friends outside of school, but Walter is the last person Ken would think someone would shoot.

"What happened?" A somber Ken asks.

"Police thinks it was a robbery," Mariah responds. "But word on the street was he was shot cause of mistaken identity."

"Are you serious?" Ken replies.

"Yeah, he looked like someone the shooters were lookin' for. They rolled up on him, opened fire. They realized he wasn't the guy they were looking for after it was all said and done," she replies.

Ken is in disbelief about what he's hearing.

"He didn't deserve this," Ken says.

"I mean, nobody doesn't deserve to be shot," Mariah replies.

"No, you not hearin' me," Ken fires back. "Walter wasn't like that. He had a full scholarship to SUNO. He was a smart dude. He wasn't involved in any street shit or anything! The man just graduated and had his entire life to look ahead to! He said he was tryin' to go to school for law, and with his intelligence, he would have had a good chance. A dude with so much potential is shot because some assholes mistook him for someone else?! It's the

Victoria shit all over again. Doesn't this bother you in the least bit?"

"Ken, we've been through this already. It's New Orleans," Mariah responds. "Shit like this happens all the time. I told you that when the shit happened to Victoria. It doesn't make it right, but it does happen."

Ken sighs, grabbing his head in frustration. The fact that this happened often enough to be acceptable made no sense to him. Walter reminded Ken of himself. He recalls a conversation they had once after a chess game. They discussed how difficult it is to go to the inner-city schools in the area, and Walter was so excited that he was in his last year. While Walter was born and raised in New Orleans, he felt he didn't fit in as well due to his good grades, which were frowned upon in the school social circles. He had big dreams when he graduated, and to hear that he died for nothing tore Ken apart. He felt if a person like Walter could get killed for simply waiting for a bus ride, what future did he have.

"What's the point of it all?" Ken says, trying to make sense of things. "I try to avoid trouble just like he did, and for what? It's only a matter of time before I get caught up."

"Ken, don't say that!" Mariah exclaims. "I'll be the first to tell you that life isn't fair, but I don't wanna hear that shit ever come from your mouth again!"

Mariah's words have little meaning to Ken, and he lies in his bed with a heavy heart. The hope of a better life fades from him as he sees no purpose of looking towards the future.

Chapter 7

Freaky Infatuation (Stevie Wonder - I Was Made to
Love Her) - 1996

The ninety-six School is out as Ken and his friends all graduated from high school in May. It's the middle of June currently, and the only thing that's on most new graduates' minds is money, and how to get it. Ken, Denise, and Shona had all taken a job with a local baseball team for the summer. Denise and Shona are working the stands selling programs to the crowd, while Ken has the job working the third base grill, which provided hot dogs and burgers to the entire park. It's a scorching hot day as Ken is sweating over the grill, turning over various patties. He's currently manning the area by himself as Mariah is on the other side of the stand, looking at her friend struggle.

"Come on, K-Dogg! Hook me up," she says, begging her friend.

"Mariah, why are you even here?" A flustered Ken responds. "You don't even like baseball!"

"I love free food though. Crazy how that works,"

Mariah quips back. "Anyway, you gonna hook me up or not?"

"No!" Ken exclaims. "Now leave me alone! You see I'm dyin' over here."

"Not 'til you hook me up," she responds as she leans on the counter.

Ken ignores her as he mans the grill making sure the chicken and burgers aren't burning. One of the main concession stand workers makes his way over to the area and checks the warming bin.

"Boss said we need another hundred burgers, fifty dogs, and fifty chickens," the worker says, causing Ken to look on in disbelief.

"Are you serious?" A stunned Ken says. "I'm here by myself!"

"Hey, don't trip on me. Get with the bosses if you have an issue," the worker responds before running off.

Ken has a look of defeat in his eyes as Mariah walks behind the counter.

"So, does that mean you can't hook me up?" She asks with a grin.

Ken shoots her an evil look before responding.

"Leave!" he grunts, causing her to jump back behind the counter.

"Well, that's not nice at all. With that type of attitude, I see why your Tallulah boo left you," she replies with a cryptic smile referring to Alisha.

She knew that would press his buttons as he turns to her with rage in his eyes.

"For that last hundred thousandth time, she didn't leave me! I broke up with her," he exclaims.

"Yeah, but that was only after your cousin told you she was cheating on you," Mariah points out. "So yeah, boo-boo, she left you before you wrote your long-ass, weak ass, break up letter."

Ken is at his breaking point as he grabs his head in frustration.

"What will it take to get you from up around here?" He says, gritting his teeth.

Mariah thinks for a moment as she checks out the menu once again.

"Two hamburgers, no, two cheeseburgers and a cold

drink," she answers with an innocent look on her face.

Ken growls as he goes into the warming bin and fixes her a couple of cheeseburgers. He hands them to her with a look of anger in his eyes.

"They count the cold drinks," he says.

Mariah smirks before taking her hamburgers and walking off.

"Thanks, fam," she says as Ken tries to calm his nerves.

He quickly turns around and starts working the grill again noticing that a couple of the burgers were burning. As he gets everything back under control, Denise and Shona walk over from working the stands still with programs in their hands.

"Hey, Ken. Did I just see Mariah over this way?" Shona asks.

"Yeah."

"What's she doing here?" She asks.

"Living up the title of 'God's Sick Joke,'" Ken replies while working the grill. "What y'all doing over here?"

"Takin' a break. That sun ain't no joke today," Shona

responds.

"Tell me about it," Ken points out. "It's only around ninety degrees to y'all. I'm over this hot fuckin' grill with no support!"

"Where's everyone else?" Inquires Denise.

"Cedric and James called in, and my sup is over at the first base tent tryin' to fuck ol' girl workin' it," Ken responds in frustration. "His ass was supposed to deliver some burgers over to her to sell, and that was like thirty fuckin' minutes ago!"

"Damn, anything we can do to help?" Denise asks.

"Nah, it's been pretty slow over this way as far as customers, thank God. I just need to get the concession stand's order in. Gonna take me all night with this shit," Ken replies as he wipes his brow.

"Look at it this way, this is the last game for this homestand. You have a week to chill and relax," Denise reminds him.

"Not for me. I got another job—a temporary one working for the week. My auntie got me this gig at a church she goes to watching summer camp kids. One of their student workers is on vacation, and they needed a person to take her place for the week. She hooked me up, so there will be no rest for me," Ken responds while removing items from the grill.

"Must be nice," Denise responds.

"For real. I guess we'll be cool sitting around the house chillin' and all," Shona says with a smirk. "You keep hustlin', Ken. I ain't mad at ya at all."

Ken shakes his head as he works the grill when his supervisor, Ed, walks over to the group.

"Can anybody drive me to the hospital?' he says to a stunned Ken. "I stepped on a nail and need to go to the emergency room."

Ken is beside himself knowing his supervisor is about to leave for the day, and he'd have to clean up and break down the grill by himself. Ed walks off as Shona and Denise make him aware that they don't have a car. Denise and Shona leave a little afterward, leaving Ken alone to run the entire third base tent on his own.

Early the following Monday morning, Ken gets off the

bus listening to his discman and starts walking down the street. He's been into some of the older music as of late and finds himself listening to the Dead Presidents Soundtrack. As he's walking down the street, almost as if it was meant to be, *I Was Made to Love Her* by Stevie Wonder starts playing when he makes it to the church and notices Brandi standing just outside of the entrance. Ken is immediately drawn to her short, dark-skinned, perfect body. As she looks around, she makes eye contact with Ken as well, as the two check each other out. Ken heads to the door with a smile on his face. He's about to approach her when Maude walks over and cuts him off.

"Are you Beatrice's nephew, Kevin?" Maude says as Brandi walks inside of the church.

"Um, yeah, but it's Ken actually," he responds.

"Oh, I'm sorry, baby. Right on time. I like that," Maude says as she led Ken into the church.

"I'm Maude, and she's told me some great things about you. Did she let you know what you'll be doing here?" She asks.

"Yeah, pretty much watching the kids during camp,"

Ken answers as he looks around the church looking for Brandi.

"Yeah, well that and handling one other special task I have for you," Maude responds as she leads him over to the hall where all the children are playing. "We normally only have girls that apply for this job, so it's especially nice to have a young man such as yourself to help with guiding our boys. Our biggest challenge is a boy named Ronald. He's older than all of our kids, and sometimes has a problem acting out."

Maude leads Ken over to Ronald, who is almost his height wrestling several of the smaller kids. Ken is stunned watching the erratic behavior by Ronald, who is bullying the other kids in the area.

"How old is he?" Ken asks.

"Fourteen," Maude replies, stunning Ken.

"Fourteen?"

"Yes. We're doing his mother a favor. Normally we don't take children that age in this program," Maude says as she checks her watch. "Well, I have a prayer meeting to attend. If you have any questions, get with Brandi over there. She'll show you the ropes."

Ken looks at the far side of the room and locates Brandi, who is sitting at a table with several of the children entertaining them. He's about to ask Maude a question, but she quickly disappears, leaving him alone amongst the kids. He's almost ran over by several of the kids who are playing in the area. Ken has never been the kid-friendly type. Even though he was the oldest cousin on his mother's side, the parents always left Tiara in charge when someone needed to watch the rest of the cousins. If it wasn't for the money, he would have already run out of the building, but getting to know the other student worker, Brandi, was also an added bonus. He finally makes his way over towards her table and smiles as she stands up and greets him.

"I see you're a little nervous around the kids," she says with a smirk.

"Nah, I'm fine. I love-"

A kid screams behind Ken, which startles him, causing him to turn around quickly. He breathes a sigh of relief before turning his attention back towards Brandi.

"Okay, maybe a little," he says as she giggles.

"So, you're the one I'm stuck with taking my girl Mia's place?" She says as she quickly checks him out.

"I guess. I'm Ken," he says.

"I'm Brandi. I guess it's just me and you for the next week," she says with a flirtatious grin on her face.

"Seems that way," Ken responds with a smile. "So, what do we do?"

"Follow me. You can leave your stuff at the table," she says as she leads Ken around the area.

As she explains the duties and their responsibilities, Ken is barely paying attention as he takes quick looks at her body when she's not looking. After explaining the job, she looks towards Ken and can tell he wasn't paying much attention.

"Any questions?" She asks, snapping Ken out of his thoughts, which is solely based on her body.

"Huh? Oh, no, I think you covered everything," he says with a smirk.

"Okay then. Well, if you need help just... oh, I forgot, did Maude explain Ronald to you?" She inquires.

"Yeah, she kinda mentioned him. Why?" A curious

Ken asks.

"Because he's your responsibility," Brandi says before Ronald catches Ken off guard and tackles him to the ground.

She looks down at Ken with a smile on her face as Ken looks up at her with a hint of fear in his eyes.

"Yeah, thanks for the heads up," he says, grimacing from pain as he tries to lift Ronald off of him.

"You're most certainly welcome," she replies before walking off.

Later that day, Brandi and Maude are walking the floor as they overlook several of the activities the kids are into. They both look outside in the play yard and notice Ken and Ronald talking with Ken holding a football in his hand. Ronald doesn't want to hear what Ken is saying and attempts to tackle Ken once again. This time, Ken is able to take Ronald down as the two wrestles on the ground.

"So, how's the new boy working out?" Maude asks Brandi.

"I think it's going well. He definitely has kept Ronald

away from the younger kids," Brandi points out, watching both Ken and Ronald rise from the ground.

Ken hands Ronald the football this time. Before Ronald can make his move, Ken tackles him to the ground. Maude nods her head with approval as she looks on at their interaction.

"Make sure he doesn't kill the boy," she says before walking off.

Brandi smirks as she walks outside to observe Ken's interactions with Ronald more closely.

"See, that's your problem," Ken says to Ronald as they both stand up. "You've been here running over little kids thinking you're big and bad. Now you dealing with me, and you can't even get a yard. Not as easy is it?"

"Man, whatever," Ronald responds, waving him off. "Give me the ball again, and I'll run you down just like everybody else."

Ken hands him the ball once more before Brandi interjects.

"Hey, fellas. How's everything going?" She says, catching Ken's attention.

She didn't have the New Orleans dialect like most of the girls Ken deals with. He can tell that she was an implant, just like he was, which intrigued him.

"Everything's cool. Just schoolin' the fourteen-year-old here on how to play football," Ken explains.

"I see. You two look like you've been rolling around in the dirt," Brandi says with a smirk. "It's almost lunchtime. Why don't y'all get cleaned up? Especially you, Ken. You have to help serve. Meet me in the kitchen in fifteen?"

Ken nods his head.

"Alright, I got you," he says before suddenly getting run over by Ronald and falling to the ground.

Brandi snickers before walking back in the church hall. Ken looks up at Ronald, who flexes his muscles.

"Told you, boy, you not ready for me," he says as Ken lies on the ground.

"You got 'til the count of five," Ken warns.

Ronald waves him off as if he's ignoring Ken.

"Five," Ken says, which causes Ronald to flee the area quickly.

He slowly rises and dusts himself off, regretting having ever taken this job. He makes his way into the church hall to clean up and prepare for lunch.

Later that day, just before quitting time, all the kids are sitting in the hall watching a movie quietly or taking a nap. Ronald, in particular, is fast asleep snoring. Ken and Brandi are sitting together, looking over the kids as Ken himself is struggling to stay awake after a hard day.

"Look at you, dozing off," Brandi says, perking Ken up.

"Huh? Oh, no it was... I just didn't sleep well last night," he responds as Brandi giggles.

"Yeah right," she says. "You can admit that Ronald wore you out. I'll have to say you were good with him today."

"The boy is almost my age in a summer camp," Ken points out while yawning. "It was easy. I probably would have acted out too if my mom had me in a summer camp with a bunch of children."

"I guess, but still, you made my job a lot easier today

taking care of him. Thank you," Brandi responded with a smile.

Ken nods his head as he takes a look at his watch and notices it's five o'clock.

"Well, I guess it's quittin' time for me," he says as he rises from his chair. "What time you get off?"

"I'm normally here until all the kids are gone," Brandi answers. "Probably will be out of here in another thirty minutes. So I guess I'll see you tomorrow then?"

Ken nods his head as he takes his Discman from his book bag and puts on his headphones.

"Tomorrow it is," Ken says with a smirk before heading out of the hall.

As he walks out of the church, he starts his CD and reflects on his day. While the day started out as a total nightmare, it ended pretty well. He enjoyed his time there and especially enjoyed the company of Brandi. He walks down towards the bus stop and takes a seat as he continues to immerse himself into his music.

The next day, Ken finds himself in the church hall

playing Uno with Brandi and several kids. He and Brandi are sitting across from each other at the little kids' table as he waits patiently for one of the kids to make their move. After the kid plays his card, Ken smiles as he puts down his second to last card.

"Uno!" He yells as Brandi snarls at him.

"Really?" She says, disgusted with Ken's bragging.

She places her card down and waits for the kid next to her to put her card down. She reverses the order sending the next turn to Brandi, who has a sadistic smile on her face laying down her next card.

"Draw four, boo," she says as Ken shakes his head. "The color is red."

Ken shoots Brandi an evil look as he draws four cards. She has a 'got ya' look on her face as she smiles, waiting for the next kid to make their move. Ken shakes his head at her as he reorganizes his cards. As he does, he's stunned when he feels someone rubbing on his leg under the table. Ken looks towards Brandi, who remains emotionless as she continues to caress Ken's leg. He is in shock as he doesn't know how to react. Brandi briefly removes her hand from his leg to play a card from her hand but goes right back to her assault moments later. She now has a sinister grin on her face waiting for Ken to play his hand.

"It's on you, boo," she says with her hand tormenting him under the table.

Ken nervously sorts through his hand and plays a card, still stunned at what's going on. He looks around to see if anyone else was noticing what's going on. Brandi playfully pinches him, causing him to jump slightly. He looks at her with confusion as she bites her lips, enjoying the feel of her victim's leg. She continues to torment his leg until she notices it's almost lunchtime.

"Alright, y'all, it's almost lunchtime. Go get cleaned up and get ready," she says with a smile as she rises from the chair and starts to walk off.

Ken is still visually stunned as the kids around him all jump up and run off to prepare for lunch. Brandi looks back and can see that Ken is confused about what just happened.

"Hey, Mr. Uno," she responds. "You coming?"

Ken slowly nods his head as he drops his cards down and follows Brandi to the kitchen to set up for lunch. He was confused with what just happened and wanted answers. Unfortunately, he wouldn't get any answers that day. Neither of them discussed what happened at the Uno game for the rest of their shifts.

Later that night, Ken is sitting in his room talking on the phone to Denise, who is laughing at him after he described the day's events. Ken shakes in embarrassment, still trying to figure out what happened.

"This shit ain't funny," Ken responds to a giggling Denise.

"Yes indeed," she responds. "Why didn't you ask her about it?"

"I don't know. The whole thing just caught me off guard. I was trippin' and didn't know what to do," Ken answers. "For a minute, I'm like maybe she thought it was her leg or somethin', but what messed me up the most is we were in a church! A place of worship! I mean, who does that in the Lord's place?"

Denise laughs once again, and Ken continues to try and make sense of it all.

"Anyway, we didn't say anything to each other for the rest of the day. I wouldn't even know where to begin with her. I didn't know that chicks could be that... I don't know, aggressive."

"They got them girls out there that will act a fool," Denise points out. "You just never came across them."

"Is that how you was when you first met Fred?" Ken says, changing the subject. "'Cause I gotta be real, I don't know what you see in that dude."

"No, I wasn't like that with him," Denise quips back. "I don't have to do all that. We been knowing each other since grade school."

"Yeah, and I get that, but eventually you passed and went on, like twice. How's he our age and still two years behind us?" Ken responds, poking fun at Denise's current boyfriend. "I mean, come on no. How can you date somebody like that? Seriously. What are those conversations like?"

"This coming from the guy who lets Mariah walk all over him, and haven't even tried to get with her," Denise fires back, causing Ken to chuckle.

"You always gotta go there, don't you?" He responds.

"You always go there with my man," she retorts.

"Yeah, but he's stupid," Ken says before his phone beeps. "Hang on a second, I gotta call."

He clicks his phone over to the other line.

"Hello?"

"Hey. Checking in on ya to see how the first day went," Mariah says.

"Hey. Baby, let me tell you what happened to me today. Give me a sec, I'm on the other line," Ken responds before clicking back over to Denise. "Hey, let me call you back."

"Must be your friend," Denise says with a giggle.

"At least she can remember my number. Your friend has trouble with numbers from what I hear, which is why he's two grades back," Ken fires back.

"Boy, bye," Denise responds before hanging up the line.

Ken clicks back over to Mariah and begins telling her the story about his first day at summer camp.

The second day of Ken's tenure with the summer camp is uneventful as he rarely saw Brandi that day since the kids were split into groups. The two shared glances, but not much else during that time. On the following day, Ken, Brandi, and several other kids and helpers are on a field trip visiting a homeless shelter. The point behind the trip was to have the kids see a side of the world they may not have encountered in their lives, but it seems wasted as most of the kids are playing around with each other instead of listening to the presentations the workers are giving as they walk around the facility. Both Ken and Brandi have to settle the kids down multiple times throughout the tour.

As one of the workers give their presentation. Brandi walks over to Ken, who is paying attention to the presentation, and begins rubbing on the back of his leg, stunning him. His eyes look left and right as he tries to do the best he can to remain calm. Brandi seems unfazed by her surroundings as she strokes her fingers up and down the back of Ken's inner thigh. Once the worker finished her presentation, she directs the group to the next room. Brandi stops her touch and follows the group, leaving Ken more confused than ever.

Back at the church hall later that evening, the kids were watching a movie as usual at the end of the day waiting for their parents to pick them up. Once again, there was no discussion between Ken and Brandi on the events that took place earlier. Ken didn't know how to approach her about it or what to say. As she stepped away to help one of the kids, Ken notices it was quitting time. He's about to leave when an idea hits him. Brandi's younger brother was part of the camp program. Ken quickly takes out a sheet of paper and writes down his name and number. He makes his way over towards Brandi's brother and hands him the note.

"Hey, give this to your sister," he tells him.

Brandi's brother nods his head as Ken puts on his headphones and makes his way out of the church once again. Stevie Wonder's 'I Was Made to Love Her' once again is playing from his disc, which reminds him of the first time he saw Brandi a couple of days ago. Realizing that the song now triggers thoughts of his co-worker, he can't help but pull out his songbook he was carrying with him once he arrived at the bus stop bench. He writes down the song with Brandi's name attached to it with a smirk.

Later that evening, Ken is sitting in his bedroom playing videogames and listening to music when there is a knock at his door.

"Come in," he says, pausing his videogame.

Jermaia walks in with the cordless phone in her hand.

"The phone is for you," she says, handing the phone to her brother.

"Who is it?" Ken questions as he grabs his remote and pauses his music.

"Some girl named Brandi," Jermaia says before walking out of the room.

"It's about time," Ken replies before walking over to his door and closing it.

"Hello," he says as he lays back on his bed.

"I heard that," Brandi says.

"Huh?"

"That 'It's about time' comment. You've been waiting

for me to call, I see," Brandi responds with a smugness.

"Hell yeah," Ken quips. "I thought your brother forgot to give you my note or something."

"Nah, he gave it to me. He said the man at camp said give this to you," Brandi responds with a giggle.

Ken chuckles as he gets comfortable in his bed.

"So, what's up?" He says, hoping to get to the bottom of things.

"I don't know, you tell me," Brandi responds, confusing Ken. "You the one asking for the call. I thought you had something you wanted to talk about."

"Well... I... I don't know," Ken responds while scratching his head with confusion. "Just trying to see what's good, I guess. I mean, you know with how we've been lately, I just wanted to see what's up with us, you know."

"What's up with us?" Brandi inquires. "What do you mean?"

Ken is stunned at this point. He can't believe she doesn't know what he was referring to.

"You know... all the hangin' out and shit," Ken

replies, trying to lead her down the path of discussion without being blatant. "I... I thought we were like gettin' real tight, for real."

"Ah, I get you," Brandi responds as Ken breathes a sigh of relief. "Look, Ken, you're a cool guy and all, and I appreciate the help you've given me. Especially with Ronald's crazy ass, but the thing is, I kinda have a boyfriend."

Ken is at a loss for words as he tries to process Brandi's words.

"Wait, what?" He responds, asking for clarification.

"I have a boyfriend," she repeats. "Sorry if I misled you, but yeah, I've been with him for about a year now."

Ken is still confused about the situation. Misled wasn't the word to describe what's been going on between the two in his mind. He never attempted to get with Brandi at all, and her blatant touching of him the last couple of days was a little more than misleading.

"Hello? You still there?" Brandi asks after several moments of silence.

"Yeah, I'm here," a confused Ken responds. "I gotta be

real here, I'm a little shocked on the whole boyfriend angle, you know."

"Why would you be?" Brandi responds, furthering driving Ken's confusion. "I mean, it is what it is."

"Yeah, I guess it is," Ken replies, shaking his head.

"Anyway, let me go. I'll see you tomorrow," Brandi says.

Before Ken can respond, Brandi disconnects the call leaving Ken more confused than when the call first started. He hangs up the line and lies in bed, trying to process what just happened. Maybe she was having issues with her boyfriend, he thought. Maybe that's what led to the show of affection towards him. Or maybe she was just crazy. After several moments, Ken sighs before starting his music back and restarting his videogame.

Day four of Ken's assignment with the church has him leading Ronald, and several other kids through the surrounding neighborhood around the church trying to sell candy for charity. He is standing curbside as the kids knock on doors trying to pitch candy to the residents. If they made a sale, they would give him the money to keep track of. He chuckles as he remembers his days selling candy in middle school, feeling he would have outsold these kids tenfold back in his day. The day has been pretty quiet between him and Brandi as she had her litter of kids to lead down the block, which Ken was fine with. After yesterday's confusing call, he didn't know what to make of her. It was nice to get out and just focus on the job at hand. His focus is short-lived, however, as Brandi's kids rush over towards his from down the block. He looks over and notices Brandi approaching him with a smile on her face.

"Hey," she says as Ken looks on confused.

"Hey. I thought you were gonna take the other block," Ken responds.

"We were, but it was boring," she responds. "I figured we'd do better as a group."

"You want all these kids ganging up on these people?" Ken responds with a chuckle. "Are you insane? It's hard enough to get sales with the few I have."

"Not really worried about it," Brandi says with a smirk. "If they buy, they buy. If they don't, oh well. At least we tried."

Ken notices the smile on Brandi's face and slowly nods his head with agreement. He knew this decision wasn't about candy. It was about them hanging out once again. As much as he was confused with their situation, he understood what she was trying to do.

"I see," he says with a smirk.

"I bet you do," Brandi quips, causing Ken to laugh.

"I thought you had a boyfriend though?" He responds.

"I do."

"So, why are you here, then?" Ken inquires.

"I'm watching my kids. Why else would I be here?" Brandi fires back.

"Your kids?" Ken responds as if he doesn't believe her.

"Yeah. Why? You don't want us along for the ride?" Brandi says.

Once again, confusion fills Ken's face as he tries to figure out his counterpart.

"No, it's cool," Ken says. "I guess it doesn't matter."

"Nope, not at all," Brandi responds with a smile.

After a few moments, the two turn their attention back

to the kids as they continue to lead them down the street. At their next stop, Ken watches as the kids go to the next house, making sure they were safe. His concentration is ruined as Brandi begins rubbing him on his leg as she stands next to him quietly. Ken looks over at her and notices the sadistic smile on her face.

"You alright?" Brandi asks when she notices his gaze.

"Am I... are you serious right now?" A mystified Ken asks.

Brandi doesn't respond as she continues to caress Ken's leg with a sadistic smile on her face. The assault finally ends when the kids make their way back towards them.

"Shall we move on to the next house?" She asks Ken.

Ken slowly nods his head as Brandi leads the walk to the next house. As they continue to make their way to each home in the neighborhood, Brandi would molest Ken's leg at every other house, making sure nobody in the group saw them confusing Ken with every touch.

Later that evening, Ken is making her way out of the

church when he notices Brandi getting into her car at the church parking lot. He didn't know she had a car and had already missed his bus since he was running late for the day.

"Yo, Brandi! Wait up!" he yells as he runs over and meets her by her car.

Brandi rolls down the window as Ken peeks in her vehicle.

"I didn't know you drove," he says.

"Yeah. This is my baby here," Brandi responds. "It's not much, but it gets me around, you know."

Ken nods his head, checking out the car. It was an older, smaller car in desperate need of a paint job. Still, it was better to have a car instead of no car. With the sun beaming down, Ken was hoping his friend would help him out.

"Hey, you mind givin' me a ride to the East real quick?" He asks.

"Oh. Well, I can't right now," Brandi responds. "I have to be somewhere, and I don't have time to make any side trips."

"Come on, it's not that far," Ken responds, pleading with her. "You don't even have to take me all the way home. Just to the next bus stop, so I don't have to transfer."

"Sorry, Ken. I can't. Besides, I have a boyfriend. What if someone sees me giving you a ride? How's that gonna look?" She responds before starting her car. "I would love to help you out, but it wouldn't be right."

Ken scratches his head as he backs away from the car. *It seems like she likes to use her boyfriend excuse whenever it was convenient for her,* he thinks to himself. She pulls off, drives out of the parking lot, and down the main street. Ken shakes his head as he puts on his headphones and makes his way down the street in the opposite direction.

Later that night, he's in his room on the phone with Denise, who is laughing at all that had happened to him earlier that day. Ken grabs his head in frustration as he's still trying to make sense of everything.

"Seriously, Denise. What is wrong with this broad?" He asks. "One minute you have a boyfriend, the next minute you harrassin' the shit out of me? This shit isn't normal at all!"

"No it's not," Denise admits with a giggle. "Why don't you just ask her about it?"

"Because that would make too much sense," Ken responds, causing Denise to laugh once again. "Naw, I hear you. You right, tomorrow, I'm gonna just flat out ask her what's the deal. It's my last day there anyway, so I might as well drop a bomb on her. I swear this is like the strangest shit ever."

"Maybe she just likes your sexy legs," Denise mocks.

"Or, maybe she's just a nut job," Ken quips back. "I mean, that seems the more likely scenario."

"Bet you five bucks you won't say nothing to the girl," Denise says, challenging her friend.

"Five bucks, huh?" Ken says as if he's pondering her proposal. "I got you. You betta have my money too."

The two continue going back and forth with each other when another call comes through on the line. Ken places Denise on hold to answer the other line.

"Hello," he says.

"Yeah, it's me," Mariah says. "What you up to?"

"Was on the phone with Denise talking about this crazy broad at the church," Ken says.

"Oh shit!" An excited Mariah says. "What happened now?"

"Hold on a sec, let me get her off the line," Ken says before clicking his phone over. "Hey, Denise, let me hit you back."

"Alright," she says before Ken swapped the line back over to Mariah to go over the day's events.

The next morning, Ken walks into the church, determined to get to the bottom of Brandi's ways. Nothing was going to stop him from getting the truth. Before he joins the kids in the hall, Maude walks over and gets his attention.

"Ken, hold up a second," she says as she walks over. "So we're going to be a little shorthanded today. Brandi called out sick today, so I'm going to need you to take charge of things today."

The news catches Ken off guard since he was determined to speak with her. Ken nods his head in agreement as Maude smiles.

"Thank you, Ken. You've been such a joy to have around this week. Come see me after you get off today so I can get you your check."

"Okay, no problem," Ken responds as he finally makes his way into the hall.

As he looks around, he can't help but feel disappointed. He notices that her little brother wasn't in attendance as well, so there was no way to get in touch with her since he didn't have her number. He takes a deep breath before walking into the hall to deal with the camp kids for the day.

As the day ends, Maude walks up to Ken and hands him a check for his week's work. It was for two hundred dollars, which was over the minimum wage.

"So, what do you think?" She asks Ken.

"Oh, this is great. Thank you," Ken replies as he folds up the check and puts it into his pocket.

"You did great work here, and I'm sure the kids are going to miss you," Maude says. "Especially Ronald. You took him off our hands for the week, and I've seen he's been a lot better with the others. Shame we can't afford to have you back for the summer, but your auntie said you had another job, right?"

"Yeah, for the local baseball team. They were on the road for the week and will be back next week," Ken replies.

"Well, if you're in the market next summer, we'd love to have you back. Tell your auntie I said hi," Maude responds before walking back into the church.

Ken smiles before walking off. As he gets to the curb, he takes a look back at the church one last time. He thinks about how odd it is that a church is where Brandi decided to do what she did. He puts on his headphones and plays Brandi's song. Unlike the lyrics, he isn't in love with Brandi, but he knows that song will always remind him of her. A smile cracks his face once more as he walks down to the bus stop.

Chapter 8

TRU Love (Outkast - Babylon) 1997-98

Ken is in his bedroom nervous as lies in his bed, getting undressed by Tanika, a co-worker of his from Toys R Us, a job he picked up several months earlier. While they weren't officially dating, Tanika took an immediate interest in him when he was hired on. Ken is a little nervous about hooking up with her as she was six years older than him, and much more experienced when it comes to sex. His parents and sister weren't home, so Tanika thought it would be a good time to try and hook up with him, and breaking his virginity before the turn of the year.

"Just relax," she says as she lowered her pants as well.

Ken nods his head but has no clue what he's doing. He's reminded of his time with Alisha, and what happened when she tried to have sex with him. He was always embarrassed by that and vowed if he were to get another chance at having sex, he wouldn't pass it up. While Tanika wasn't necessary Ken's type, she isn't a bad looking person to have sex with. She dark-skinned, short, and not a bad shape, to say the least. Ken is surprised about her stretch marks on her stomach and how loose her skin was. He has never seen a stomach as loose as hers was. He recently found out that she had children when he went over to her house after work a couple of weeks back. She had two kids at her home and showed him a picture of a third one. She had lived a life prior to them getting together, but that didn't matter in Ken's eyes for the moment. What mattered is him taking advantage of the opportunity he is about to experience.

Tanika mounts him once she's dropped her pants and panties, and tries to insert him into her. The only problem was Ken's manhood wasn't cooperating with her.

"I told you to relax," Tanika says again. "If you're not relaxed, this ain't gonna work."

"I am relaxed, see," Ken responds as he lays his head back and closes his eyes. "How relaxed do you want me to be?"

Tanika sighs as she continues to struggle to get Ken's member working properly. After about ten minutes of getting nowhere, she finally gives up as she dismounts him.

"Maybe we need to try it at another time," she says, disappointing Ken.

"My bad. I've never done this before, so I'm not sure of what I'm supposed to be doin' right now," Ken explains as he gets out of the bed and locates his underwear.

"Haven't you ever watched porn or somethin'?" Tanika asks.

"Of course, it's just... I don't know, it seems different than that," Ken responds, putting on his pants. "My bad. This is just crazy, for real."

Tanika smiles as she finishes putting on her clothes. She walks over and kisses Ken before collecting her purse.

"Feel like ridin' to my place?" She asks.

"Sure, I guess. Let me get my uniform and shit so I can just catch the bus by you to the store," Ken replies as he quickly goes into his closet and grabs his things.

As the two exit Ken's home, he's stunned to see Jermaia making her way home. A sudden feeling of relief overcomes him. He could have been caught having sex in his mother's home if she had walked in. She's still surprised to see her brother walk out of the home with Tanika as he slowly approaches her.

"Hey, what are you doin' here?" He asks. "Thought you had cheerleading practice today."

"It was canceled," Jermaia responds as she takes a look at Tanika. "So, who is this?"

"My friend, Tanika. I'm about to head to work a little early, so let mom know when she gets home," Ken says, trying to dismiss Tanika's presence as much as he can.

Jermaia isn't buying Ken's excuse as she folds her arms, trying to get the truth from her older sibling.

"So, you're just allowed to have friends in your room when momma ain't home now?" She says with a hint of attitude.

"Wasn't in my room. Anyway, I'm outta here," Ken says as he quickly leads Tanika away from his sister down the street.

Tanika smiles and waves at Jermaia as Ken quickly pulls her away.

Later that night, Ken is on break from work and is

standing outside of the store talking with Shona, who had stopped by to visit him. She's laughing as Ken explains what had happened with him and Tanika earlier, causing him to lower his head in shame.

"Oh my god," she says as she wiped tears from her eyes. "That is too funny."

"Yeah, well not all of us have that experience like you," Ken points out, alluding to the fact that Shona already had her first child.

"Baby, wait 'til I tell Mariah about this!" Shona exclaimed, catching Ken off guard.

"Whoa, wait a minute," Ken says, waving her off. "Under no circumstances do you tell Mariah about this shit. I don't wanna hear her mouth, for real."

"Why? It's not like y'all are fuckin' or something," Shona points out.

While it's true, he and Mariah weren't together, she always had this weird protective understanding about Ken. While she wasn't into Ken as he was into her, she would always fuss at him if he ever had any progress with any girl. He never directly asked her to be with him in a relationship sense, but she knew he wanted to get with her, and would always change the subject if she felt it was leaning to that. Still, he tries to hide any relationship from her as best he can to avoid her jealous rage, which coincidently actually turned him on slightly.

As Shona and Ken continue their conversation, Ken's coworker, Bryan, joins them outside in front of the store. Shona is immediately taken with him as his blue eyes stood out to her. He was of a middle eastern background and had a small goatee on the bottom of his chin.

"Yo, Ken. What's good?" he says as he daps his coworker off.

"Ain't nothin', man. These damn Tickle Me Elmo's are driving the fuck outta me," Ken responds as Bryan leans on the wall next to him. "I mean, why these people gotta get nasty every time we tell them it's not in stock? Just crazy to me, for real."

Bryan nods his head as he checks out Shona, who smiles at him.

"Since my friend here is rude as fuck, let me introduce myself, I'm Bryan," he says as he approaches Shona.

"Hey, I'm Shona, Ken's friend," she responds, making sure to emphasize that she and Ken have a platonic relationship.

"Well, it's nice to have friends," Bryan replies with a smile as Ken can see what's going on.

"Yeah, well, break time is over for me. I'll holla at you later, Shona," Ken says as he stretches.

"Yeah, I gotta get goin' too," she responds. "Call me tonight when you get off."

"Girl, I might be in here 'til early in the morning," Ken warns.

"That's fine, I'll be up. Make sure you don't forget," she says before smiling at Bryan one last time. "It was nice to meet you."

"You too," Bryan responds with a smirk.

They both watch Shona walk to the bus stop before making their way back into the store.

"So, what's up with you an ol' girl?" Bryan asks as he follows Ken back into the warehouse.

"Nothing. Just a friend," Ken responds.

"Well, if y'all just friends, why don't you hook me

up?" Bryan responds with a sinister grin. "Do your boy a favor."

"She has a dude," Ken points out as he puts his smock back on. "And she just had a child not too long ago by said dude. Trust me, you don't want them issues."

"Just slide her my number, and see what she says," Bryan responds as he puts on his smock and follows Ken to the back of the warehouse.

They make it to a secluded area in the corner of the warehouse where Ken had stashed some comics and candy he had taken from the floor. The area was blocked off by several big ticket items that hid from both cameras and other personnel, allowing Ken and the other warehouse workers to hid from management. Ken laid down on one of the baby mattresses located on the bottom shelf of the area, as Bryan took a seat on a power wheels box.

"Alright, it's your funeral," Ken says, agreeing to give Bryan's number to Shona. "I don't ever mess with another man's woman. That's a rule of thumb. Fools act crazy about their women out there. Especially when they have a child together."

"You saw how she was lookin' at me," Bryan bragged. "Trust me, I'll kick a lil' game to her, and we'll be straight."

Ken shrugs as he starts reading one of the comics he had.

"So, what's up with you and Tanika?" Bryan says, trying to gossip. "You tap that ass yet?"

"Nah, not yet," Ken responds as he munches on a few gummi bears.

"Aw, come on, fool. Everyone knows y'all hookin' up outside of the job. Surprised you ain't tear that ass up already. You not a virgin, are you?"

"Hell no!" Ken exclaims, becoming defensive.

"Well, then get to it, partna," Bryan responds. "If you don't jump that ass, I'm sure there are a few dudes workin' here that will."

Ken waves Bryan off as he goes back to his comic. While he acts as though he's not concerned, he is confused about what he needs to do to actually lose his virginity.

After a long night, and early morning of working, Ken

walks into his house around three in the morning. He's exhausted as he makes it into his room and plops down on his bed. Just as he's finally able to breathe, his phone begins to ring. He now has his own personal phone in his room, so nobody else in the home is disturbed by the ringing. It still was strange for the phone to ring at such a late hour. Ken picks up the line, almost confused.

"Hello?" he asks.

"Who in the hell you out there tryin' to fuck!" Mariah exclaims, surprising Ken.

"Mariah?"

"Don't play fuckin' stupid! Who is Tanika?" She fires back.

Ken grabs his head with frustration as he knew exactly where she found out about his coworker.

"Well... she's... she's just my coworker," he explains. "How did you know I was-"

"I heard she's twenty-four with five kids," Mariah fires back.

"No. Well, it's three kids. It's not a big deal," Ken explains, trying to calm the situation. "I don't know what

Shona told you, but-"

"No big deal?! Are you out of your mind," Mariah responds. "How could you possibly entertain the thought of being with that scallywag?"

"Scallywag?" A confused Ken repeats. "You know what, never mind. Look, I'm just hangin' out with the girl? I think you're looking way too-"

"I bet you two up in there having sex and doing all kinds of freaky shit, ain't you?" Mariah fires back.

Ken sighs and grabs his head in frustration once again. He was not in the mood to have this discussion after the long day he's had.

"Hello?! You bet not have hung up on me!" Mariah exclaims after Ken didn't respond to her promptly.

"No! Christ, I'm still here," Ken responds.

"Getting' all quiet and shit," Mariah responds. "I bet she's teachin' you all kinds of new shit, ain't that right?"

Ken sighs as he knew that she wouldn't let her finish his sentence regardless of what he had to say.

"Look, it's late, and I think you're-"

"She bet not be teachin' you nothing new!" Mariah

exclaims.

Before Ken can respond, Mariah hangs up the phone. The entire conversation has Ken confused as he scratches his head before hanging up the line.

"God can't be this bored," he says to himself before getting undressed from his work clothes and jumping under his covers.

Typical Mariah tactic, he thinks to himself. Once she acts as if they're together, Ken would loosen up and come back to her, only to be put on the sidelines. He isn't going to let her disrupt this hook up this time. He is determined to make things work with Tanika.

A couple of weeks later, Ken, along with Shona, Denise, and Bryan, all walk into the home of Mariah's Aunt for Mariah's birthday celebration. The home is packed from wall to wall as the DJ hypes up the crowd with the local bounce music New Orleans is known for. While the apartment is a decent size, it's nowhere close to being able to hold as many people that were in attendance. Ken never liked big crowds and was always uneasy when faced with them. He notices Mariah, who is entertaining other friends in the party wearing a mock princess crown with pinned money draped down her shirt. She notices Ken and his crew and quickly makes her way over.

"What's up, y'all!" Mariah exclaims as she hugs both Shona and Denise before sharing a hug with Ken.

"What's up, Mariah. Happy birthday," Ken says. "This is my coworker Bryan. I hope it's cool I brought him by."

"Nah, it's cool. The more the merrier," Mariah says as she checks out how close Shona and Bryan were. "Well, I think there's some food left in the kitchen and some drinks. Y'all help yourselves."

Shona and Bryan nod as they quickly make their way to the kitchen. Mariah chuckles as she turns to Denise and Ken.

"So, am I missin' something here?" She asks as she leads Ken and Denise to a seating area. "I mean, Shona is still with Rahiem, right?"

"Yep," Ken replies.

"Well, does she know that?" Mariah replies with a smirk.

"Yep," Denise answers.

"Alrighty then," Mariah says as she tries to fan herself to cool off. "So, Ken. Why didn't you bring your new boo to the crib?"

Ken laughs and shakes his head.

"You know good and damn well I ain't bringing nobody around you," he responds. "I don't need them type of issues in my life."

"I was about to say, you bet not bring that scallywag around me!" Mariah exclaims.

"What does that even mean?" A confused Ken responds. "Nobody talks like that! What were you a pirate in another life?"

"Don't try and change the subject," Mariah fires back before turning her attention to Denise. "Denise, you met his new boo? She's a scallywag, isn't she?"

Denise shrugs, attempting to stay out of the discussion as Mariah turns her attention back towards Ken.

"See, she don't wanna say, but I know the type you like. Just like your fast ass girl this summer," Mariah points out.

"Oh shit. I forgot to tell y'all about church girl," Ken says as he snapped his fingers, referring to Brandi. "Picture I saw her in one of my classes in UNO."

"You lying," Denise responds with a smirk.

"I kid you not. She didn't even speak to me. Acted like she didn't even know me," Ken responds.

"Maybe you should have shown her a little leg to get her excited," Mariah jokes as she and Denise laugh.

Ken shakes his head with embarrassment and is about to walk off when Mariah and Denise pull him back down. The trio continues their discussion amidst the party crowd laughing and joking the night away.

After the party, Ken, Denise, and Shona are led by Bryan into his home. The house is huge as Ken can immediately tell that Bryan comes from money.

"Parents are out of town, so go ahead and chill," Bryan says as he walks into the massive living room.

Ken and the others are impressed as they look at the big screen TV in the room. They take a seat on the comfortable couch and are blown away.

"Oh my god," Shona says. "This has to be the most comfortable couch I've even sat in."

"For real," Ken affirms. "And what size is this TV?"

"I don't know," Bryan answers. "Yo, Ken, help me get some drinks real quick."

Ken nods his head as he follows Bryan towards the kitchen area. Once there, he pulls Ken to the side.

"Say, can you run interference with Denise?" He asks. "I'm trying to show Shona the whole house, you feel me."

Ken cringes at the thought of Bryan hooking up with Shona.

"Dude, a little too much info," he responds. "Me and Denise cool. Do what you gotta do."

"Cool. Appreciate it, bro," Bryan says before handing Ken a few drinks. "You should try and get with Denise, for real."

"Get with Denise? Why would I do that?"

"Dude, I know you then checked out them big ass breasts of hers," Bryan answers with a smirk. "I'm just sayin', you then told me about Mariah and how y'all thing ain't goin' anywhere. You ain't tapped Tanika's ass yet, so why not hook up with Denise? I'm gonna go start the movie and take Shona on a tour. That should give you more than enough time to run up in that ass."

Ken is hesitant, to say the least. He shrugs as he and Bryan make their way back to Shona and Denise. Ken hands Denise and Shona the drinks, as Bryan takes out a laserdisc, and loads it into the player. He cuts the TV on as the movie starts. He shares a glance with Shona, who smiles and nods.

"Say, me and Shona are gonna be right back. I wanna show her my music collection," Bryan says as Shona rises from the couch. "There's a whole bunch of movies over there if y'all get bored."

Bryan and Shona quickly make their way out of the living room as both Denise and Ken shake their heads.

"Why didn't they just say they about to fuck?" Denise inquires.

"For real," Ken replies. What are we, like ten?"

Denise giggles as they get comfortable in their seats to watch the movie.

As the movie continues, Ken finds himself peeking over, trying to see Denise's breasts. He never noticed them before, but Bryan was right, they were a nice size. He chuckles to himself as Denise looks at him confused.

"What's so funny?" She asks.

"Oh, nothing. Just had a thought, that's all," he replies before turning his attention back to the movie.

The two friends continue to watch the movie together in complete silence as Ken's mind starts thinking about his options.

It's quitting time on New Year's Eve at Toys R Us as Ken, Bryan, and Tanika all walk out of the store. There's a little nip in the air, but it's not too cold as the three co-workers are all talking.

"Yo, you sure it's cool that I come through to the party?" Bryan asks.

"Sure. My people don't care who comes," Ken responds. "The thing is, I know you and Shona then had y'all's little fallin' out. She's gonna be there too. I don't want none of that drama at my crib."

Ken was referring to the breakup between Bryan and Shona that happened two weeks prior. It got messy when Shona and her friend came over to Toys R Us and flattened Bryan's car tires. According to both, the beef between them was over, but Ken knew how Shona is and knew she wasn't done with it. Bryan nods his head with understanding as he walks over to his car.

"I promise you, I'm not gonna disrespect your house," Bryan responds. "I'm thinking about bringing Nicole with me too."

"Really? Nicole?" Ken says with a sly grin. "Damn, she ain't been here for like a week, and you already with that?"

"Nah, I'm just trying to get down," Bryan says as he opens his car door. "Probably won't stay too long though. Think we gonna take a ride after we ring in the new year."

Ken and Bryan chuckle as Tanika shakes her head in disgust.

"Y'all are sick, for real," she says as she enters the back seat of Bryan's car.

Both Bryan and Ken share a laugh before getting into

the car and pulling off.

Just before midnight, the New Year's Eve party is in full effect at Ken's parent's home. There's music playing with several family members dancing and plenty of food for all the welcomed guests. On the far end of the living, Shona is frowned up as she looks over towards Bryan and Nicole dancing with each other. She's sitting next to Rahiem, who is on his fourth drink of the night. Ken is sitting in between Denise and Tanika, watching everyone dance and enjoy themselves. He's spending more time laughing and joking with Denise which has Tanika feeling some type of way. She's about to mention something to Ken when Shona suddenly walks over to him.

"I want him to leave," she says folding her arms.

"Who?" Ken inquires.

"Bryan, that's who! I don't want him here!" Shona responds.

"Why? What did he do?" Ken says as he stands up and looks towards Bryan and Nicole.

From what he can tell, they are enjoying each other and

not causing any issues with anybody.

"I mean, he's just over there dancing. What's the issue?" Ken asks an almost offended Shona.

"Look, if you don't tell him to leave, I'm gonna tell him," she fires back.

Ken sighs as he knew she wasn't lying. Shona is known for causing scenes since high school, and he didn't want to upset his family's celebration with unnecessary drama.

"Fine, I'll take care of it," Ken responds as he makes his way through several family members before approaching Bryan and Nicole.

"Hey, Ken. Thanks for the invite," Nicole says with a smile as her petite body swayed with the music.

"Hey, no problem," Ken says while scratching his head. "Yo, B, can I get a word real quick?"

Bryan nods his head as he walks over to the far end of the dining room with Ken.

"Look, Shona over there trippin'," Ken explains. "She wants you to leave. I know, it's bullshit, but you know how she gets with shit."

Bryan looks a little disappointed but understands

where Ken is coming from.

"Alright, I'm cool with it," Bryan responds. "It's almost midnight. We'll bounce after the countdown. Cool?"

Ken daps Bryan off before both of them return to the party. Shona immediately walks overlooking for an update.

"Well?" She says with an attitude.

"He's gonna bounce after the countdown," Ken says. "It's about five minutes 'til. After that, he's gone. You happy?"

Shona wasn't too pleased as she wanted Bryan gone at this very moment, but she nods her head with understanding.

"Fine," she replies before walking back over to her boyfriend, Rahiem.

Ken shakes his head as he takes a seat between Tanika and Denise again.

"Everything cool?" Denise asks.

"It's Shona," Ken points out with a smirk. "Ain't shit ever cool with her."

Shona continues to mean mug Bryan from a distance. He, in turn, acts as though he's having the time of his life as he dances closely to Nicole, making sure that Shona can see every move.

Five minutes later, everyone in the house is on their knees praying before the year's end, which is tradition with Ken's family. After the clock strikes midnight, everyone rises from their knees and celebrates wishing everyone they come in contact with a happy new year. Tanika is surprised when Ken hugs Denise before her, but remains silent about what's she's been noticing throughout the night. Shona is hugging Rahiem but has her eyes fixed on Bryan as a scowl enters her face watching him and Nicole kiss from a distance. After a few moments, Bryan walks over and daps Ken off before waving at Denise and Tanika. He and Nicole make their way out of the home shortly afterward. Ken breathes a sigh of relief as he looks towards Shona, who seems satisfied.

An hour later, Ken and his crew all are in his bedroom enjoying themselves. With Bryan gone, Shona has even loosened up as they are entertained by Rahiem's jokes. He's had way too much to drink as everyone seems tired. Tanika is laughing as well, but she keeps an eye on Denise and Ken, who are whispering to each other. She knows she's going to have to address the issue later, but for now, she keeps it to herself.

The next morning, after a night of partying, Ken and his crew are passed out in his room. Notably, Ken and Denise are lying on his bed, while the others are scattered throughout the room on the floor. Tanika yawns as she wakes up and notices Ken and Denise are lying in bed together. They weren't under the covers or anything, and Denise was laying at the foot of the bed and Ken was at the top. It didn't matter to Tanika, however, as she knew it was time to address the situation. Before she can say anything, Ken's father knocks on the door, walks in and checks out the room.

"Good morning," he says as everyone wakes up. "Anyone need a ride home?"

Ken yawns as he rises from the bed along with Denise. He's shocked to see that she was with him in the bed. He looks towards Tanika and can tell that she's upset about something. The couple doesn't say anything as Ken leads her, Denise, Shona, and Rahiem out of his room.

Later that day, Ken is back in bed, trying to catch up on his sleep lost from the night previous when his phone suddenly rings. He yawns for a moment before ignoring the phone and turning over in his bed. The phone continues to ring, which irritates Ken. After a few minutes, a frustrated Ken leans over and picks up his phone.

"Hello," he growls.

"Why you takin' so long to pick up your phone!" Tanika exclaims on the phone.

"I don't know, probably because I'm sleep!" Ken fires back as he lies back down in his bed. "What do you want?"

"I wanna talk about last night," Tanika responds. "And how you all in your girl Denise's face!"

"What are you talkin' about?" a confused Ken says before yawning.

"You and Denise. I mean, it's pretty fuckin' obvious!" Tanika exclaims. "What's up with that shit last night! Y'all were in bed together? I'm your fuckin' lady, and I'm sleepin' on the floor!"

"Okay, first of all, you need to calm your ass down," Ken responds, becoming agitated. "You wake me up with this bullshit?! I didn't know the girl was on the bed. I fell asleep just like the rest of y'all! I woke up just like you did and noticed it. Can't believe you woke me up with this shit!"

"Bullshit!" Tanika responds. "It wasn't even just that! You spent all night talkin' to her! Then, soon as New Year's hit, you hug that bitch instead of me? Are you fuckin' serious right now?!"

Ken grabs his head as he's confused with what Tanika is talking about.

"I don't know what you trippin' on, I really don't," Ken responds. "But if you feelin' some type of way, then you can go 'bout your business 'cause I can't deal with this shit. Don't know where none of this is comin' from. Me and that girl are friends. Nothing else. If you can't deal with that, then you can bounce!"

Ken abruptly hangs up the phone and turns off his

ringer. He's heated by the accusations Tanika was making, but in the back of his head, he wondered about Denise. He remembered how Bryan had mentioned her before as being someone he should look into. Ken never gave it any thought before that comment. His goal was to eventually get with Mariah, but seeing how things weren't progressing as he would have liked, maybe it was time to entertain the thought of Denise. After a few moments, he yawns before turning back over to try and get some sleep.

A few days later, Ken and Mariah are sitting at Burger King, enjoying their meals while talking. Ken was explaining all that went down at his New Year's Eve gathering between Shona and Bryan, which has Mariah's full attention.

"Oh my God," she says before taking a quick sip of her drink. "Shona know she be out there, for real. I heard she slashed his tires and everything. Is that true?"

"Yep. I was talking to her in the store, and like minutes after she left, Bryan came to me pissed off over the shit," Ken explains. "Apparently, one of her friends was with her. They did the deed. Who does shit like that? Especially when she was in the wrong. I mean, she's the one with a man messin' around and gets mad at ol' boy. It's crazy for real."

"I see that. If you wouldn't have invited your scallywag over there, I might have come through," she responds with an attitude.

"Well, you don't have to worry about my scallywag anymore," Ken responds, still trying to understand where she got that term from. "We broke up the day after. She's been mean muggin' me at work these last couple of days. Probably runnin' her mouth about me and shit."

Mariah looks as though she's surprised.

"Really? When was you gonna tell me about it?" She asks.

"I'm tellin' you now," Ken responds. "Shit just wasn't workin' out."

"I guess. Or maybe it was because you couldn't get it up," Mariah responds with a smirk. "I'm just sayin' maybe she was a little frustrated with you. You ever think 'bout that?"

Ken shakes his head, filled with embarrassment.

"Damn Shona," he responds, causing Mariah to giggle. "You ever think about how she tells you all my business, but she never speaks on her shit to you?"

"Of course she's not. In her eyes, she's perfect," Mariah points out. "Besides, I need her to tell me, 'cause it's clear you wasn't ever gonna tell me about the girl. Well, she has three kids, so I guess girl is the wrong label for her. I'll continue to go with scallywag. That suits her, on the real."

Ken sighs as Mariah giggles once more.

"So, what song is she?" Mariah asks.

"What makes you think she has a song?" Ken quips back.

"Fool, you then told me you have a song for damn near everybody and every occasion," Mariah points out. "If you not gonna tell me what my song is, you can at least tell me what her song is."

Ken thinks for a few moments. Mariah was right, saying he had a song for everyone. He told her about his songbook years ago, and he was stunned that she still remembers it. She was always good about listening to him and picking up on little things like that. Still, he did get further along sexually with Tanika than anyone else. She was deserving of a song just for that.

"I don't know," he responds to his friend while she's eating her fries. "I honestly didn't think of one for her, but I do need to come up with one."

"I got the perfect one," Mariah says with a sinister smile on her face. "You remember on Friday when Craig's girlfriend pulled up? They was playing that 'You ain't nothin' but a hoochie mama' song. That's her for real. Hoodrat, hoodrat, hoochie mama!"

Ken bursts into laughter as Mariah starts rapping the song.

"Girl, you need to quit," Ken responds still laughing. "I am not gonna do that to that girl."

"Why not? I mean, it's not like you ever gonna tell her about it," Mariah points out. "And I swear if you ever tell her about her song, and you didn't tell me about my song, I'm gonna beat both y'all asses."

"Yeah, yeah, whatever," Ken responds, brushing off

her threats. "I'm thinking more along the lines of Outkast. Babylon."

Mariah looks at him strangely.

"Babylon? I ain't never heard that one," she says.

"I mean it's not a whole song that talks about it, but there's a verse that goes something like 'we explorin' each other's privates until we felt excited then, ah. It's on from here on out. Put your hands in the atmosphere if you know what I'm talkin' about'," Ken recites further, confusing his friend.

"How does that have anything to do with either of y'all?" Mariah asks. "I mean, you explored shit, and it didn't work, remember?"

"It doesn't necessarily mean we… you know what, never mind," Ken responds, shaking his head. "Can't believe you got higher grades than me in English. Not everything is what it sounds like. Metaphors and shit, you know."

"More like meta-whores when you talkin' 'bout her," Mariah quips with a smirk. "And don't even start on English grades. I know more than you think."

Ken chuckles as he balls up his wrapper. He and Mariah were two of a kind, and the only people who understand them are them. Despite Mariah's jabs, Ken decided that it was the perfect song to describe he and Tanika's brief relationship. In some ways, he was happy he wasn't able to fully have sex with her. The fact that she had three kids at such a young age was telling on how fertile she is. He could have had child number four with her, which was a scary thought. It wasn't his time yet, but will Mariah be the one who allows him to cross that threshold? What about Denise? All these questions are flowing through Ken's head as he enjoys his discussion with his friend. One thing is for sure, it wouldn't be Tanika.

Chapter 9

Crossroads (Mary J Blige - Seven Days) - 1998

Four months later, Ken is lying in his bed talking on the phone with Mariah as he's trying to wait for the right moment to discuss their future together. He's been in a constant battle within himself trying to decide his next move. In the months following the New Year's incident, Ken had found himself another job working at a call center after things between him and Tanika broke down. The situation had gotten to the point where they almost had an altercation on the store floor. He also distanced himself from Shona as things between the both of them started to sour. For the first time in his life, he felt some sort of control, which was something he had never felt since moving to New Orleans. Still, the one thing he is missing is a girl to call his own, and it was time to put the pressure on Mariah. While he found himself hanging out more and more with Denise, he still couldn't let go of the first New Orleans girl he ever had a crush on. As always, Mariah found ways to dance around the subject.

"Come on, Mariah," he says, talking on the phone. "I'm trying to see what's up with us. You keep saying this and that. I'm tryin' to see what's up for real."

"What's up is that I like where things are, and so do you, so we're good," Mariah fires back. "Now that we've settled that, what you got going on tomorrow? Mom gonna put some greens on. Wanted to know if you wanted to stop by."

"You know good and damn well I don't like greens," Ken responds. "And quit changing the subject. Ain't nothin' settled about this."

"Ken, come on now. We-"

"No, let me finish real quick," Ken responds, cutting her off. "We've been around and around with this thing for a minute now. I mean, what else do I have to prove here?"

There's silence on the line, which is a first for Mariah. She could chat her way out of anything, but the fact that she went silent caught Ken off guard.

"You still there?" He asks.

"Yeah, I'm here. Look, I'm just gonna be real, Ken. I don't know about that whole relationship thing right now," she admits. "I mean, if you're into someone like you say you are, you should be able to wait on them, don't you think?"

"Mariah, I've been waiting," Ken replies, happy that he's finally getting somewhere. "I mean, come on. I think I've done my part in this."

"You have been patient. I'll give you that," she responds. "I get it. We've been friends since you was talkin' all white and shit. You still talk white to me, but at least it's passable in the hood."

"Mariah," Ken says, trying to keep her on track. "What's the problem with us being a thing?"

"I don't know, Ken. I'm... I... look, I'm just not ready for that right now. I mean, I'm not sayin' it won't happen, but for right now, I just need you to be a little more patient. I promise you when the time is right, I'll let you know," a sincere Mariah responds.

Ken sighs because it's not the answer he was looking for. He's about to respond when his line beeps.

"Hey, hold a sec. I got another call," he says before switching lines.

"Hello?"

"Hey, it's me. What you doin'?" Denise says.

"Nothin' much. Just talkin' on the phone with Mariah," Ken answers.

"Oh, you want me to call you back?" she asks.

Ken thinks for a quick moment before responding.

"Nah, hold on a sec," he says before clicking back over to Mariah.

"Hey, Riah. Let me call you back," he says.

The line is silent.

"Hello, Mariah? You there?"

"Yeah, I'm here. Okay, I'll holla at you later," she says.

It was the first time Ken had ever got off the phone with her to talk to anybody, which caught Mariah off guard. He was at a crossroads. His choice was to either take Mariah up on her word and wait, hoping that eventually she would be on the same page as he was, or explore life without her. He felt a little out of his comfort zone. He knew he might have made a big mistake, but the hold she had on him had to be severed one way or another. He also thought that by separating from her, she would come to her senses sooner rather than later.

"Hey, Denise, you still there?" Ken asks.

"Yeah, I'm still here," she responds.

"Hey, what's up?"

"Nothing. Just wanted to see if you wanted to run to the mall this weekend," Denise responds. "I need to find a Mother's Day gift. You did your shopping?"

"Hell naw," Ken responds with a chuckle. "I'm a last-minute shopper. My mom is out of town this weekend anyway, so I have plenty of time."

"Cool, then pick me up tomorrow so we can knock this out," Denise responds.

"Alright, I'm down," Ken says. "So, what else is going on?"

He and Denise continue their conversation gossiping on whatever they've heard throughout the week. While Ken was enjoying the conversation, in the back of his mind lingered Mariah, and the decision he made.

The next day, Ken and Denise are making their way through the crowd of people who have filled the mall to purchase last minute mother's day gifts. As they pass several stores, Denise points out several items that Ken refuses. They stop at one store and checks out a purse that is on display in the store window. Ken cringes as he takes a look at the price before shaking his head in refusal.

"Oh, come on. You know that's nice," Denise says, trying to convince Ken to purchase the gift.

"For that price, it better get up and dance," Ken says, causing Denise to laugh. "I'm serious. Ain't no way I'm paying that for a damn purse."

"Not even for your mama?" Denise inquires.

"Trust me, there's a good knock off guy up in here somewhere. She'll never know the difference," Ken answers as he and Denise continue to make their way through the crowded mall.

"Some son you are," Denise responds.

"I'm working part-time at a call center right now. With what they're paying me, she's lucky she's getting anything," Ken points out.

"Don't make no sense to be that cheap," Denise mocks.

Ken chuckles as he thinks to himself for a few

moments. He decided he would see what was up between Denise and someone she had an interest in.

"So, I've been meaning to ask you, what's up with you and ya' boy?" He says, catching Denise off guard.

"Who? Allen?" Denise responds.

"Yeah, y'all two ever hook up?" Ken inquires.

Allen was someone both he and Denise went to school with. He was her version of Mariah, someone she was interested in but couldn't get to where she wanted to get with him.

"If by hook up, you mean sex, then hell no. That boy ain't payin' me no never mind," Denise responds.

"I mean, if you really wanted to get that, you need to show a little more ass," Ken jokes. "Seriously, that's what dudes wanna see. Take it from me."

Denise shakes her head with a smirk. Ken notices something in a nearby display window.

"Wait, here we go," he says as he led Denise over. "Now you see, that's what I'm talking about. This is the perfect Mother's Day gift."

Denise looks at the tacky t-shirt that has 'Happy

Mother's Day' written on the front of it. She cringes before turning her attention towards her excited friend.

"So, what do you say?" Ken asks.

"Oh uh-uh," she replies. "I'm not gonna let you buy your mother this ugly thing!"

"It's ten dollars though," Ken responds, pointing out the price tag. "You can't beat that."

Ken is about to walk into the store when Denise grabs him by his arm and leads him away. The two continue down the mall once again as Denise decides to get some information of her own.

"So, what's up with you and Mariah?" She inquires.

"Not a damn thing," Ken answers. "She just loves to send out mixed signals and shit. I don't know what she's trying to do, for real."

"Still leavin' you hangin'?" she responds.

"Yeah. It's crazy 'cause I'm cool with her not wanting to be with me, but then the second I try to move on, boom, she's on my ass fussin' and cussin'," Ken says. "I mean, you're a girl. What's all that about?"

"Okay, first of all, I'm a woman, not a girl, so check

yourself," Denise responds playfully. "Second, not all women are alike, so I can't answer why she does what she does."

"Get outta here," Ken responds with a chuckle. "All y'all monthly bleeders are the same. Y'all are just crazy, not knowing what y'all want. Don't act like you're any different."

Denise looks at Ken strangely.

"Did you just call me a monthly bleeder?" She asks.

"Yeah. All y'all are," Ken confirms as Denise shakes her head.

"Baby, with statements like that, you really wonder why Mariah don't want you?" Denise says with a snicker.

"I don't talk to her like that," Ken points out. "Seriously, what's going on with her?"

"I don't know. Me and her ain't cool like that," Denise responds. "Only time I used to talk with her is when I hung out with her and Shona."

"I thought y'all were cool up in school," Ken replies. "You don't keep in touch?"

"School was school. I don't talk to half the people I

went to school with," Denise responds before taking a look at Ken. "Hell, I don't know why I continue to talk to your ass."

"Cause I'm one of your few friends who actually has a car," Ken points out, causing Denise to laugh.

The two check out several more stores trying to figure out the perfect gifts for their mothers while continuing to discuss their relationship struggles.

Later that evening, Ken and Denise walk into Ken's home with several bags in their hands. Ken places the bags on a nearby coffee table before taking a seat on the living room couch. Denise takes a seat next to him as he turns on the TV.

"What I told you," Ken brags. "Cheapest Mother's Day gifts in the city. Told you we'd get everything we needed for cheap."

"You were right, damn," Denise replies with a smile. "Is that what you want to hear?"

Ken nods his head with a confident smile as he switches channels on the TV. The two get comfortable as they try to find something to watch on TV.

A few hours later, Ken and Denise are sitting on the living room floor eating pizza and watching the movie Eraser on TV. Ken cringes as he watches the horrible movie action.

"This is such bullshit!" Ken exclaims. "I mean, come on! Look at that big ass alligator! Arnold should have been dead like a hundred times already!"

"Why you gotta take everything so seriously?" Denise inquires. "It's just a movie."

"Movie or not, they gotta make it a little realistic," Ken responds.

"If you don't wanna watch it, change the channel," suggests Denise before finishing up her slice of pizza.

"Ain't nothing else on. Besides, it does have Vanessa Williams. Might as well get a few lustful looks at here since I'm watching it," Ken responds, causing Denise to roll her eyes.

As they continue to watch the movie, they both reach for the two-liter soda that was sitting between them touching hands in the process. Both Ken and Denise glance at each other as an uneasy silence fills the room.

"Oh, my bad, I didn't know you was gonna get some," Ken says as he removes his hand from the bottle.

"No, it's all good," Denise replies as she removes her hand as well. "You can go first," she says.

Both of them look at each other, as something as simple as a touch causes the two to rethink their friendship. Their thoughts are short-lived as they move in and begin kissing each other. After a few moments of passionate kissing, the two grasp each other and are rolling around on the floor, making out with each other. Denise starts to undress, which surprises Ken, who starts to unbutton his pants as well. The two continue their make-out session as Denise leads the intercourse. She was the more experienced having had sex previously, and she can tell the Ken doesn't have a history with such things. Unlike with Tanika, Ken is aroused and Denise is able to insert his manhood inside of her as she mounts him. The warmth of her body has Ken in a state of bliss as he closes his eyes. The feeling of passion has Ken overwhelmed as Denise starts to grind on him. His moment of passion is short-lived as Ken starts moaning loudly, successfully having his first official orgasm. Denise looks at Ken strangely as the process was only about thirty seconds. Ken is breathing heavily as confusion fills his eyes. If Hollywood has taught him anything, it is that sexual intercourse should last a lot longer than what he just experienced. As he opens his eyes, he notices Denise staring down at him.

"Um… So," Ken says, trying to come up with something to say.

"Yeah," Denise responds as she's just as speechless.

"I mean… what just happened?" Ken asks.

"I… I don't know," Denise says as she removes Ken's member from her, and rolls to the side.

Ken is a little embarrassed as he quickly gets dressed, still trying to figure out what happened between the two. The recent connection between the two friends seems a little awkward as Denise gets dressed as well. The two remain silent as they turn their attention back towards the TV watching in silence, not knowing what to say or how to react.

Later that night, Ken walks back into his home after dropping Denise off to her home. He walks into his room and lies on the bed. It was an awkward night after their sexual interaction. The two friends tried to talk around the issue earlier, but they both knew that what happened between them changed their relationship. Ken sighs before turning over and looking through his collection that was located next to the bed. After a few moments of searching, one CD catches his eyes. He loads the CD into his radio and skips to track seven before getting back into bed. The song that plays is 'Seven Days' by Mary J, Blige. He closes his eyes as he lies on his pillow, replaying the night's events in his head over and over again. Sex was new to him, and he didn't know how to react to finally breaking his virginity. He'd always pictured in his head having the sex for the first time with someone he was in a relationship with, more specifically, Mariah. The encounter with Denise came from left field, and although he was clueless on how to proceed with their friendship, it felt right.

A small smirk enters his face as he opens his eyes, reaches under her bed, and pulls out his old songbook, which is showing a lot of wear and tear. He writes Denise's name in the book, followed by the song of the moment 'Seven Days.' Just as the song states, he and Denise made love, and he wasn't sure about what they were going to do about it going forward. He looks over the book for a moment as he always does when entering a new item before placing it back under his bed. He takes his radio remote and skips back to the song once again, wanting to relive the moment between him and his friend once more.

A few weeks later Ken is in his room playing videogames and listening to his music. In the weeks passed, Ken and Denise hadn't talked much. When they did talk, it wasn't about what had happened that night between them. Ken figured if she didn't bring it up, he wouldn't bring it up, and maybe things would go back to normal until he could figure out what he wanted to do next. While playing his game, his phone rings. He quickly answers the phone and balances it on his shoulder as he continues to play his videogame.

"Hello?" He answers.

"Hey, it's me," Denise says.

"Hey, what's up?" Ken says, trying to focus on his game.

"Hey, so I um, I need to talk to you about something," Denise answers.

"What happened?" Ken asks. "Is this some more Shona drama, 'cause I told you that girl is off, for real?"

"No, it's nothin' about that. Look, so there's no easy way to say this, so I'm gonna just say it. Ken, I'm pregnant," Denise responds.

Ken chuckles as he continues playing his videogame.

"Girl, what are you talking about?" He says not taking her seriously. "Why you call messin' with me like that?"

"I'm not messin' with you," Denise responds as Ken pauses his game to give her his full attention.

"Are you fuckin' with me?" Ken inquires once more. "This shit ain't funny if you are."

"No, Ken. I'm serious. I'm pregnant," Denise responds again as a nervous Ken finally takes her seriously.

"Pregnant? But... but how?" he responds nervously. "We only did it the one time!"

"That's all it takes, Ken," Denise replies.

"Are you sure? Did you take a test?" Ken questions.

"Several of them."

Ken sighs as he never thought that he would be in this predicament at such a young age. He's quiet as a million thoughts are running through his mind, including how was he going to break the news to his family.

"You still there?" Denise asks, breaking Ken's concentration.

"Yeah… I'm… I'm here," Ken murmurs. "So… well… what… what do we do now?"

"I don't know. I've never been through this," Denise answers with a hint of uncertainty in her voice.

"Have you told your parents?" Ken asks.

"Just my mother," she responds.

"Wow… I'm just… at a loss for words," Ken responds. "A kid. I'm not even in my twenties yet. I don't know if I'm ready to be a father."

"Well, baby, get ready 'cause the baby is comin' whether you're ready or not," Denise responds.

Ken grabs his head in frustration as one night of

pleasure has just changed his entire life.

Chapter 10

Gettin' Grown (Mary J Blige - Share My World)

1998-99

It's early in the morning as Ken is sitting in the room half sleep, holding his daughter, Danielle, in his arms. He yawns, struggling to stay awake and feeding his daughter. She's just under three months old, and Ken is struggling to adjust to being a parent. Danielle normally sleeps in four-hour intervals, which has him dizzy at times. Luckily with his new job, he only works three days out of the week, and on those three days, Denise cares for the baby. Ken yawns once more as he logs into his computer and chats with a few folks online while cradling his daughter. Although he's exhausted, he looks at his daughter's face and smiles. He thinks back to when he first moved to New Orleans, and how rough it was for him to adjust. With all the stress and classmates he lost due to jail or violence, he figured he'd be next somehow and was just waiting for the day that he too would die. However, Danielle changed things in his eyes. She gave him the motivation to better his life. He wasn't just living to die anymore; he was living to make sure she would survive. Even his mother noticed his more upbeat attitude since she's been born. It was a struggle for him, but he made it work the best way he knew how.

A few days later, Ken is getting Danielle's stuff together when his mother knocks on his bedroom door and enters.

"Hey, Mariah is at the door," she says to a confused Ken.

After Denise's pregnancy announcement, Ken and Mariah took a step back from each other. Now that Ken was a father, and attached to Denise, Mariah didn't want there to be any confusion on her part. Denise was the one person Mariah never gave Ken a hard time about. Still, he wasn't expecting her. He checks on Danielle in her swing before walking out of his room to the front door. Mariah greets him with a smile as she has a gift in her hand.

"Hey," she says.

"Hey yourself. What's up? I didn't know you were stopping by," Ken responds.

"Yeah, my sister had some business out this way, so I decided to stop by and say hi," she responds.

Ken looks outside and notices Mariah's sister sitting in the car. They wave at each other as Ken turns his attention back to his longtime friend.

"So, is this a bad time?" Mariah asks.

"No. Well, I was just getting ready to go drop off Danielle to Denise's house, but I'm good," he responds. "Come on in."

Mariah walks into the home as Ken leads the way to his room. Once inside, Mariah is blown away as she walks over to the baby's swing.

"Oh my god, she is so cute," Mariah says as she crouches down, looking at Danielle with a smile. "I'm so happy she takes after her mother, for real."

"Yeah, you ain't never seen my baby pictures," Ken points out. "She looks just like me. You wanna hold her?"

"Oh, I don't know. I'm always nervous dealin' with kids," Mariah responds as she stands up. "By the way, this is for you."

She hands him a gift bag, which is filled with a few

outfits and other baby items.

"Thanks. I appreciate it," Ken responds before putting the bag on his computer desk. "Come on, lil' scary. Sit on the bed, I'll bring her to you."

Mariah is nervous as she takes a seat on the bed. Ken takes Danielle out of her swing and hands the baby to his friend, who looks a little uneasy.

"See, that's not hard. Now is it?" Ken points out.

Mariah looks at Danielle once again and smiles at her, still overtaken by her beauty.

"You did good, Ken, for real," Mariah responds. "Never seen you as a father type, but you look like you holdin' it down."

"You should have seen me before," Ken responds before taking a seat in his computer desk chair. "I didn't know how to change a diaper, fix a bottle... hell, I didn't even know how to open the can of formula for the baby. Shit was embarrassin'."

"But you did it," Mariah points out. "I mean, I know it's still early on, but you did what a lotta dudes won't do. You took care of your responsibility. Most of the dudes I know are dead beats. Won't even acknowledge their kids, let alone raise them. And I'm not even mentioning the kids who grew up without a father 'cause he's locked up, or shot dead in the streets. This here is something beautiful, and you did good."

Ken sighs as he shakes his head in disagreement.

"I did what I was supposed to do," he responds to his friend. "I don't look at it as doin' good."

"That's because you still got that Kansas in you," Mariah jokes with a smile. "We have a lot of kids growin' up without dads in the hood. Trust me, you may not know it, but you should be proud of what you are."

Ken thinks for a moment before slowly nodding his head in agreement. He still didn't think what he was doing was anything special, but he did appreciate Mariah's sentiments. He notices Mariah is still a little uneasy holding the baby. He smiles as he rises from his seat and takes the baby off her hands.

"Thanks," she says with a smirk. "I still can't believe you and Denise hooked up. Shona was pissed 'cause she didn't know about it."

"You don't know the half of it," Ken responds with a chuckle. "She knew I was at the house one day, and knew I was with her, and kept calling my line. I'm talkin' the phone must of rung thirty times. When I finally answered, she damn near cussed me out for not tellin' her, and then said she was gonna tell you before hangin' up on me. That girl ain't right."

"She's really not," Mariah says with a smirk. "That's your friend though, so that's on you."

"Oh, now she's my friend?" Ken responds shaking his head. "I wouldn't even know the chick if it wasn't for you. But that's neither here nor there now. Don't know why she was so pissed at me and Denise hookin' up anyway."

"Because she lived in a world where the only person she was satisfied with hookin' up with you was me," Mariah responds, thinking about Shona. "It was always me and you in her eyes. Remember at my auntie's wedding where I caught the bouquet, and you caught the garter. I showed her the picture of us from then, and she said it was destiny and shit. Honestly, I didn't know what to think myself that night, but that's the reason she was so upset.

Well, that and the fact she's throwed off."

Ken laughs as what a lot of Mariah was saying was true. He also felt the same way, thinking that the two were destined to be together. He eventually learned that life doesn't follow what he feels is destiny.

"Yeah. Wasn't long ago where I was just as crazy as she was when it came to that subject," Ken admits. "Funny how things work out."

"Yeah, it kinda is," Mariah replies.

Both are silent for a moment before Mariah looks at her watch.

"Well, I guess I need to jet. I'm sure you have to get your daughter to Denise's house, and I got my sister out there waiting. It was nice to see you again, Mr. Kansas," Mariah responds as the two embrace.

"Nice to see you too, Ms. Project," Ken jokes. "Don't be a stranger."

After a few moments, they back away from each other and share one last look. Ken leads her to the living room and opens the door for her. He watches her get into her sister's car. They share one final glance as Ken waves at her. Mariah smiles and waves back as the car pulls off down the street. After a few moments, Ken looks at Danielle, who is nestled in his arms.

"Alright, you, let's get you to your momma house," he says with a smirk.

The smile on his face is short-lived as he takes a whiff of her.

"Really, Dani? Really?" He says, looking at her.

He sighs as he walks back into the house to change his daughter.

Six months have gone by as Ken and Denise are finally able to get away from their parental responsibilities and spend some time alone. After attending a wedding earlier in the night, they decided to take a detour to a motel to stretch out their night just a little bit longer. It wasn't the best of places, but it was the only place Ken could afford that charged by the hour. The two have just finished having sex as Ken looked at his watch and noticed they still had about twenty minutes left. He lies down in the bed once again with Denise lying on his chest as they relax for a bit.

"This is cool," he says with a smirk.

"What is?"

"Just layin' here. I'm pissed off that we gotta go back," Ken responds as he thinks for a moment.

"Yeah, this is nice. Would be nice to lay together all night, not worrying about going anywhere," Denise agrees. "Laying in our room with Danielle's crib beside us. It'd be like a real family."

Ken thinks for a few moments before sitting up in the bed.

"What if we did just that?" He proposes. "You know, we get our own place away from our parents? It's just me, you, and baby girl. Get us a nice apartment. It would be perfect."

"Baby, you know good and well your folks ain't gonna go for that," Denise says as she rises from the bed as well. "Plus, we would need furniture and stuff like that. We don't have that type of money. At least I don't."

"You forget what's coming up in a couple of months. Tax time," Ken reminds his lover. "We have a baby this year. Now, you haven't worked this year, but I have. If I claim the baby on my taxes, that's a chunk of change that's gonna come my way. I hear how folks with kids get a lot back. Maybe we would too. With that, we could get all we need to start off."

Denise thinks for a moment before shaking her head with disagreement.

"I don't know. It seems like we'd need a lot more than tax money to pull that off," she replies. "I mean, it sounds nice, but I don't know if we're ready for all that."

Ken chuckles as he gets out of the bed and begins getting dressed.

"Sometimes you have to just take a chance," Ken responds. "Besides, how's that old sayin' go? I need to make an honest woman out of ya. If we were to do this, we couldn't do it out of sin as the old folks put it. We'd have to do it as husband and wife."

Denise is in the process of getting dressed as well when she stops in her tracks and turns her attention to Ken.

"Did you just ask me to marry you with a bunch of old people clichés?" She asks.

"Well, I figured if we are going to move in together,

we should at least entertain the idea of marriage," Ken responds as he buckles his belt. "Look, I don't wanna be one of those couples who do the whole baby mama and baby daddy thing. I wanna do this the right way—mother and father living in one household together. Danni is about to make one in a little bit, so she's gonna start remembering shit and learning at a quick pace. I would rather her learn it in our place, not back and forth."

Denise takes a deep breath as she ponders Ken's proposal.

"Just think about it. Is all I ask," Ken says as he puts on his shoes.

After a few moments of silence, Denise nods her head with agreement.

"Okay," she responds with a smile. "Let's do it. I'm down."

Ken is stunned because he didn't think she'd answer him so quickly.

"You sure about this?" He asks, now feeling doubt.

"Yeah, I'm sure. Why? Are you not sure?"

Ken chuckles as he walks over and kisses his bride to

be.

"We're fuckin' nuts. You know that, right?" He says.

"Hey, it was your idea. If it all falls apart, it's on you," Denise jokes.

The two share a glance for a few moments before Ken looks at his watch once again.

"Girl, hurry up and get dressed before these people run through here tryin' to kick us out," he says as Denise quickly gets dressed.

Ken and Denise pull up outside of Denise's home, parks and shuts it off for the moment. Not much has been said since the proposal from earlier. This was a huge step for both of them, and neither knew how to proceed.

"So, are we really doing this?" Ken asks.

"I was about to say the same thing," Denise replies. "When should we tell our folks?"

"When we're already married and moved in," Ken replies jokingly. "Honestly, at this point, they shouldn't expect anything different from us. We're grown now. High school seems like it was a lifetime ago. It's our life. We make the choice, not them."

"Fine, so let's tell your folks first," Denise responds as she folds her arms.

"Well, I'd thought we'd practice with your people first, and then figure out how to tell my folks," Ken responds, causing Denise to laugh.

"Oh, uh-uh," she replies. "We not gonna practice on my people. You think you slick!"

"Fine, fine. Let's just get them together or something, and do it together," Ken proposes. "At least then we can get it all out, and listen to the fifty thousand speeches of how we're not ready."

"Fine, I can do that," Denise responds. "There's only one thing I'll need. The ring. You have it?"

"Christ, I didn't plan this out," Ken admits with a chuckle. "I literally thought about this when we were lying in bed."

"Well, before we do anything, you need to get the ring," Denise responds. "That way, it'll be real. To our folks, and me."

Ken ponders for a moment before slowly nodding his

head.

"Alright. I don't know much about this stuff. And I don't have like a thousand dollars for a ring and all," Ken responds. "So it's gonna probably be a cheap Walmart ring. Is that cool?"

"Ken, it's not about the money," Denise advises him. "It could be a crackerjack ring, as long as it's real and it comes from the heart, I'll take whatever you give me."

Ken smiles as the two share a kiss before Denise hops out of the car. Ken watches her until she's safely inside before starting the car and pulling down the road.

A couple of weeks later, Ken and Denise, who is wearing her new engagement ring, are at Ken's home standing in the living room across from both of their parents, who are sitting the couch. The room is quiet as the two friends turned lovers have announced their intentions to marry each other. Ken and Denise remain quiet, waiting for some reaction from their parents.

"Do you have a plan?" Denise's mother asks. "Is there going to be a wedding? And if so, how are you going to pay for it?"

"We decided to skip all the extra. We'd rather spend our money on getting an apartment," Ken explains.

"And do you know what all that entails?" Ken's mother asks.

"I mean, we've looked into it. There's a spot not too far from here. It works in our price range, and it covers rent and utilities. Even though we're not planning on doing this for a couple of months, I called, and they said they have vacancies," Ken explains as if he's under interrogation.

"What about furniture, food, and other necessities?" Denise's mother responds. "It's not just about rent. There are so many things that go into it."

"Mom, we've looked into it," Denise responds. "We're waiting until tax return time. With Danni on Ken's return, we should be pretty good. We're gonna use that to get us going."

"That's right. Plus, I already have a little saved up, so I think we'll be fine once we get started," Ken chimes in. "I know what y'all are thinkin', but me and Denise got this. I just think it's best that we have a spot to call our own. We just wanted to get y'all together to let y'all know our plans. We're gonna do it regardless. We hope y'all approve."

Both Ken and Denise's mothers look at each other with a hint of concern as Denise turns her attention to her father.

"So, dad, what do you think?" She asks.

"Yeah, dad. Anything you'd like to add/" Ken says to his father.

Ken's dad scratches his head, not having anything to add to the discussion.

"Long as you take care of your family, I'm fine," he responds.

"Yeah, son. Welcome to the family," Denise's father responds as he rises and shares a hug with his soon to be son-in-law.

Ken looks confused as Denise shrugs. Both of their mothers are still showing signs of concern, but eventually, rise and hug their children as well, accepting their soon to be union.

"So, y'all not gonna have a wedding or anything?" Ken's mother asks.

"Can't afford it," Ken points out. "We'll probably just

go down to the courthouse and do that. It's cheap, it's quick, and it makes it legal, which is all we need."

"Well, y'all at least need to have a reception," Denise's mother responds. "That way you can get gifts that will help start y'all off in the new house."

Ken and Denise look at each other because neither had considered that option.

"Okay, that makes sense," Denise responds.

"We have a lot to get together between now and then," Ken's mother points out. "Let's work out the details."

Both Ken and Denise nod their heads in agreement as they finally take a seat to discuss the details of their forthcoming marriage. They both take a quick look at each other and are relieved since neither of them anticipated the response they were receiving. It seems like their parents are behind them all the way, which put them at ease for the moment.

It's Friday, and the wedding morning, as Ken is asleep in his bed in his parent's house. Since announcing the engagement, he and Denise have found them an apartment they were set to move into on Monday. Ken took the following week off to help get his new place together. It's been a struggle, but today is the big day. Ken is sound asleep in his bed when his radio alarm goes off. It starts playing a rap CD that comes on silently at first before it blasts gunshot sounds causing Ken to jump up and fall out of his bed.

He rubs his head as he rises to his feet.

"Damn, I gotta stop leaving Pac CD in the radio at night," he says as he sits back on the edge of the bed.

He's about to lay back down when his telephone suddenly rings. He yawns before picking up the line.

"Hello?"

"Hey, just makin' sure you up," Denise says.

"Yeah, I'm up," Ken says while lying back down in the bed.

"Good. Having second thoughts?" She asks.

"No. You?" He responds.

"No. So I guess we're really doin' this?" Denise replies.

"It would seem that way," Ken says before a thought

enters his mind. "Anyway, let me get going. I got some stuff I need to take care of before the courthouse. I'll see you there."

"Okay. Don't be late," Denise says before hanging up the line.

Ken hangs up the line as well before he follows up on his thought, goes under his bed and pulls out an old shoebox. He opens the shoebox to reveal items filled with memories from the past, including his songbook. He smiles as he pulls out an old cassette tape. He puts the tape into his radio and plays it.

The tape starts by playing 'Please Don't Go, Girl,' which brings back memories of Sharon from middle school. He laughs, thinking about the thirty-second relationship he had with her as he looks through an old yearbook with her photo. He also looks at the drawing of the heart she gave him on their final day together. He thinks back to how innocent he was at the time, and how he thought he never would have found anybody after that. That drawing was a symbol of no regret, and for the most part, he lived up to that the best he could.

The second song that comes on is 'Rush Rush,' which reminds him of his first girlfriend, Hilary. While things didn't end so pleasant for the two, she would still always be his first official girlfriend. He chuckles at the water balloon fights they had that one summer, and before the whole racial issue, he enjoyed her company.

The next song, 'Iesha,' brought back memories of his first unofficial wife, Iyesha. He remembers spending time with her and her friends. He ponders if she would approve of his blackness now. While the song seems childish now, it also reminded him of a time where he felt his first real racial incident. It changed the whole dynamic of his life and opened his eyes to a lot of things he hadn't seen before. Remembering Iyesha's smile before she left his life for good still lights up Ken's face when he thinks about it.

The next song hit Ken hard as the song 'If I Ever Fall In Love,' reminds him of his first New Orleans crush, Mariah. Outside of Denise, Mariah was the one girl in his life that changed him the most. She saw the transformation from a Kansas kid to a New Orleans man. He never could fit in with the rest of the city as even with his schemes with

Denard and Toon, he could never be one of them. Still, as much as Mariah mocked him at times, she always looked out for him and was one of his best friends even though they were never in a relationship with each other.

The following song, 'The Sign,' reminded Ken of a tragic time of the attack on Victoria. He had hoped he would have seen her again in a store or out and about somewhere, but it never came to be. He sighs reminiscing on how frightening it must have been for his old friend to go to a school that rejected her because she was white. He never wanted to forget that moment as it reminded him of the harsh reality of the racial separation he witnessed. He really tried to help her fit in, but in the environment she was in, it was never going to work out no matter what he did.

The next song picks things back up as Ken is reminded about his time in Tallulah, where he experienced his first kiss from Alisha. 'Street Thing' starts to play as Ken takes hold of the plush bear Alisha had given him all those years ago. Ken is embarrassed when he thinks back to the 'almost-sex' situation between the two of them. She was a good kisser, and Ken is just taken aback by the memories of the old skating rink in the small country town.

Up next on the playlist was 'I Was Made to Love Her,' which immediately caused Ken to laugh at the thought of his old freaky coworker, Brandi. This is still the strangest thing he had encountered up until that point. In the back of his head, he would always ponder what her angle was. She never admitted why she did what she did, but the mystery was what made her such a character. Ken had a high standard to assign anyone a song in his book, but this was the one exception. He only knew her for a week, and in that week, she made a lasting impression that the Stevie Wonder song would always remind him of.

As the next song is played, Ken takes a deep breath as 'Babylon' begins to play. It was Ken's second attempt at sex, which failed miserably. He lowers his head with embarrassment once again when something hit him. Since his first encounter produced his daughter, maybe it was destined that all attempts prior failed. Tanika already had three kids, so she was as fertile as they come. Had she and Ken completed their sexual act, it would have been devastating to his future. Ken chuckles while thanking God that their encounter ended the way it did.

Ken's first sexual act with Denise, however, was a different experience altogether. 'Seven Days' pretty much described it as after the deed was done and they didn't know what they were going to do. It changed their friendship forever, and from their brief interaction came the child that had given Ken hope after he had lost it. It was the most important event to happen to him.

After the song goes off, Ken thinks for a moment after reminiscing over the past. The memories of past love covered only eight short years, but in those eight short years, Ken grew up from a young, naïve boy to a headstrong man. Life wasn't fair, and he made a lot of mistakes in the past, but by going down memory lane, he knows for certain that he is making the right choice marrying Denise. One thing bothered him. He needed a song for the moment, one he had hoped would close out the songbook in regards to loves of his life. He thinks for a few moments, checking out his CD collection struggling to come up with a perfect song. After a few moments, a big smile enters his face as he finds the perfect song. He quickly loads the CD into the player and selects the track. In his book, he writes Denise's name in there once again, followed by the song that would signify this day forever in his heart. He writes 'Mary J. Blige – Share My World' in the book while he engulfs himself with the song.

"Hell of a fuckin' ride," Ken says to himself as he closes the songbook and enjoys the music.

Today was the beginning of the rest of his life. Before he made the commitment of a lifetime, he wanted to reminisce about his past experiences. He wanted to see what molded him to the man he had become. After the song is over, he lies in his bed silently and takes a deep breath. After several moments, he rises from his bed, ready for the rest of his new life.

Check out more great E. Nigma readings at:

www.enigmakidd.com

To submit a manuscript to be
considered, email us at
submissions@majorkeypublishing.com

Be sure to LIKE our Major Key

Publishing page on Facebook!

CPSIA information can be obtained
at www.ICGtesting.com
Printed in the USA
LVHW091742271020
669964LV00004B/930